Praise for T/

"...I thought abc ... ... more than that; it is different but especially so and in that sense stands outside of comparisons. Vastly original, this is something entirely new."

—The BookBeard's Blog

"...a perfect example of seamlessly writing multiple genres together. Definitely recommending to sci-fi, horror, and fantasy fans!"

—Hayla, @BookLovingCatMom

"There is a great depth of culture, species relations, and atmosphere in this story and I really want to read more in this world."

—William C. Tracy, author of the Biomass Conflux series

Praise for *They Eat Their Own*

"A good read, much like the first book. I'm really enjoying the layered characters and colorful world these authors created..."

—@MissPark84

"And it's a hell of a lot of fun. I love this world, I love these characters, and I can't wait until King and Swanson give us book three."

—Bryan S. Glosemeyer, author of The Shattered Gates series

"Dockhaven ... is so well described, you can practically smell the sea salt and feel the wind blowing the stink from the slums. The dichotomy of high tech and low fantasy really shines through, and creates such a unique setting. You really do get a feeling of a hive of scum and villainy, with a thin veneer of gentility over it."

—Steve Caldwell, The Bookwyrm Speaks

Novels by King & Swanson

A GOOD THIEF

A GOOD THIEF

a Thung Toh jig prequel

AMANDA K. KING &
MICHAEL R. SWANSON

978-1-7335783-8-7 (paperback edition)
Library of Congress Control Number: 2023945621

Edited by Glen Hollow, Ink. and John J. Wikman
Cover painting, *Badger's Luck*, by Michael B. Fee
Cover design by Amanda K. King with Euan Monaghan
All photographs by Michael R. Swanson unless otherwise credited

Printed and bound in the United States of America
First printing October 17, 2023

Published by Ismae Books
contact@ismae.com
Indianapolis, IN 46219

ismae.com

Dockhaven Map Key

❶ Big Island tram station
❷ Keepers of the Brine Temple
❸ Seers Abbey
❹ Estoan Lodge
❺ Mucha Hall
❻ Integrated Zoetics secret lab
❼ Dockhaven Desalinization Plant
❽ Marthoth Air & Sea Warehouse 4
❾ Slaughteryards
❿ Pukatown
⓫ Keepers of the Brine Chapel
⓬ The Runoff
⓭ Tendle's Marine
⓮ Ooda's cuddy, Itnee's Pastries
⓯ Bathhouse
⓰ The Bag
⓱ The Bitter Barnacle
⓲ Lower Rabble tram station
⓳ Order of Omatha
⓴ Tenta's Fish Fry
㉑ Spriggan Temple & Orphanage

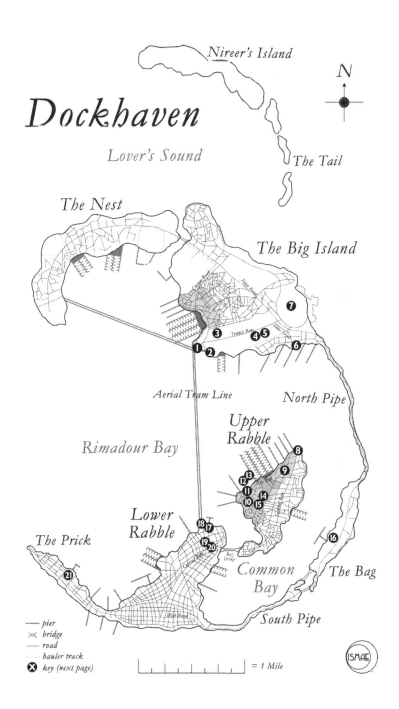

Dockhaven

Nireer's Island

The Tail

Lover's Sound

N

The Nest

The Big Island

Aerial Tram Line

North Pipe

Rimadour Bay

Upper
Rabble

Lower
Rabble

The Prick

Common
Bay

The Bag

South Pipe

pier
bridge
road
hauler track
key (next page)

= 1 Mile

ISMAE

Ismae: The Known World

Ukur

Cloviist

Dominion of
Chiva'vastezz

Twilight Sea

Dockhaven

Middle Sea

Republic
of Eita

Haasteboah

The Nors

Castling Sea

Leaky Sea

'ehtaemah

Empire
of Oras

Sea of Dawn

ISMAE

© Amanda K. King &
Michael R. Swanson 2019

The Calendar

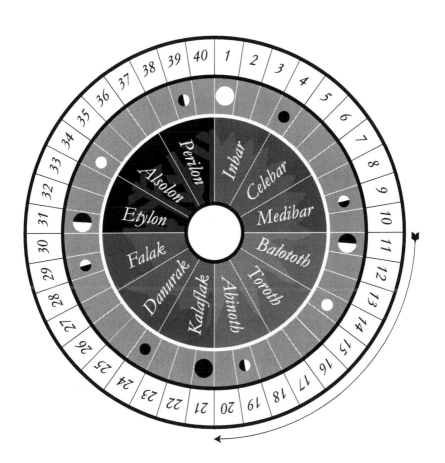

SCHMALCH

2085 MEDIBAR 13

The rain had stolen his chances tonight.

Schmalch leaned out from under the tram entryway and glared at the sky. He was a good thief—he just hadn't had many opportunities this evening. Nobody wanted to be out on a dark, drizzly night like this.

He really wanted a brew and a warm spot to drink it, but his last two coppers had gone to a street vendor for this morning's meal—and Garl wouldn't let him inside the Bitter Barnacle without coin in-hand. In the years since being kicked off the barkeep's filcher crew, Schmalch had tried sneaking in, faking it with a handful of stones, even slipping behind the bar and pouring one for himself, but Garl had always gotten wise. So, Schmalch had been outside all day, watching commuters, searching for an open pocket, a dangling purse.

Late morning, when the rain blew in, he'd given up his gloss spot in the alley between the Order of Omatha and the dross shop with a name Schmalch couldn't pronounce. Owing to daytime shift changes and nighttime tipplers, he scored five or six times most days from that perch. But people didn't like to carouse in the rain, especially this chilly late-spring stuff. Every tram-load that let off was half as full as it would have been on any dry day. Even worse, when it rained people put on more clothes, hiding their pockets and purses.

High above, he heard the clank of the tram car coming into the station. In a few heartbeats dozens of footsteps were clumping down the stairs. Schmalch crouched in the blind spot by the newel post and waited as the commuters' steady rhythm grew louder, closer. It sounded mostly like the larger species—karju, chivori, he couldn't distinguish—all their footsteps like thuds in comparison to the patter of puka feet like his.

Waiting for the marks to make their way down the many flights was the worst. He could have worked the lift exit, but too many gutter babies hung out there begging and filching—and many lift riders were rhochrot, four-legged and so huge Schmalch couldn't reach their purses without being trampled. Plus, the Corps had posted someone there recently because some toff from the Nest got their guts spilled while slumming in the Rabbles last quartern. Working the stairs took patience, but it was dry and reliable.

At last, a broad karju man stepped into sight, body covered by a rain-slick poncho. Their grey faces hidden by hoods, a pair of chatting chivori women followed, but they held their bags tight against their bellies in an attempt to keep the dosh inside dry. The karju woman who came next wore a broad-brimmed hat against the rain, her waist-length jacket flaunting the bulging purse at her belt.

When she paused to adjust the hat, Schmalch crept forward—hoping the surrounding noise covered the squelching he felt in his shoes—and reached for her purse. Before his fingers could touch it, the woman strode into the street, hat doing its job.

Schmalch slumped back into his blind, sure he was doomed to spend the night copperless and damp, when a final passenger appeared. Wearing only a light sweater, the chivori man paused under the awning, swore at the rain, and stooped to tie his shoe. His purse wasn't fat, but it was handy. Schmalch slipped in close. With a gentle tug and a slash from his kris, the leather bag slumped into his palm. The man straightened, and Schmalch leapt back into the shadows, barely able to hold off opening his boodle until the mark was gone.

With a dozen coppers in hand—enough to drink all evening and still enjoy a morning meal—Schmalch pulled the frayed collar of his coat over his head and scuttled into the street. The rain soaked through before he'd taken ten steps.

As Schmalch turned the corner onto Anchorage Way, Sigrin Malpockey passed under a streetlamp in the distance. The minikin was with a few of his compas, all of them in their stupid rat-fur boots. Schmalch ducked into the nearest alley and waited for them to pass. A couple months back, what had started as a chance to join Sigrin's crew had turned into a failed catnapping and a debt for the lost ransom. Twice since then, the bully'd had his thugs hold Schmalch for a beating. Each time, Sigrin took what little coin Schmalch had and added to his debt. If they saw him now, he'd lose the day's boodle, get punched in the gut, and still owe two Callas, if not more.

"… of a sister," Sigrin said as he approached the alley. Schmalch froze, not even breathing. "I mean, something like that. How dumb does she think I am?"

"Dunderpate quim," one of the tall cronies said.

"Lash that down right now." Sigrin stopped at the mouth of the alley and jabbed a finger up toward the thug's fat nose. He might have been a minikin karju, but he was as mean as any of the big ones.

Schmalch sunk deeper into the shadows. Sigrin wouldn't see him, he assured himself, wouldn't smell him. He'd been the orphanage's scour the shadows champion, one time staying hidden for nearly two days before Elder Sriree found him in the cellar when she came down for canned goods. Times like this, he wished he'd never graduated, could go back to the Temple of Spriggan after a rotten day of scaling. Maybe he could be an elder some day and teach the gutter babies instead of being one.

Sigrin's voice pulled him back, "She's *my* bitch sister. I get to say things like that about her. *Not you.* You think she'd ever pay us if she thought I let you lot talk about her that way?"

The thug shook his shaggy blonde hair. "Apologies, Sig."

"You're right, of course." Sigrin started walking again, the other Grey Boots following like street cats shadowing a rat. "She really is a dunderpate quim, but only I get to say it. Understood?"

Schmalch waited until he could no longer understand their muttered agreements and apologies and hurried on, breaking into a full run when he saw the lumia-algae glow of the Bitter Barnacle's sign: *Drinks Dancers Food.* Dripping and shivering, Schmalch ducked inside. Enough bodies filled the room to make it warm—though the damp from outside still seeped through the building's every hole and crack. Schmalch had spent too many days swabbing mold and mildew from them all.

When he smelled Schmalch, Garl looked up from his work and pointed a thick finger to the exit. Schmalch waggled the purse. The big bartender jerked his chin and went back to washing mugs.

Schmalch scurried down to the far end of the bar. It was uncomfortably close to the dartboard, but the humongous jar of fruit soaking in liquor was down there. It was a great blind. Some nights, Garl forgot him for hours. So, Schmalch took the risk of being jabbed with a wayward dart and climbed onto his favorite stool.

On stage, a curvy karju dancer moved to the thudding, mechanical beat of the melody engine. Schmalch spotted three crews who were fresh into port—one or two were usually good for a lift. They'd go half-seas over and forget how much they spent. A few were eating soup—tonight's special, probably made from leftovers from a few nights back. Schmalch had once helped Garl make soup from cast-off bones left on plates.

Finished with the other patrons, Garl walked down to Schmalch and grunted.

"One brew," Schmalch said. "A big mug of the cheap stuff—and a bowl of tonight's soup."

Garl tucked a towel into his waistband. "Show me the coin first."

Schmalch opened little the leather bag and displayed his loot. Garl plucked coins from the purse, filled a mug, and thunked it down in front of Schmalch.

"I'll be back," he said and walked away.

Schmalch sipped and scanned the crowd. Garl's filchers were already working the room, but that didn't mean they'd spot all the possibilities.

"Is that you, Schmalch?" Ooda slipped out of a cluster of people.

Before he could answer, she'd climbed up on the stool beside him, somehow keeping her slinky pink dress in place. It looked pretty against her dusty-green skin. She'd worn cosmetic—a line of red dots above her big brown eyes, a matching stripe down the arc of her nose, her lips painted a darker green than her face. She always looked so pretty.

"It is you," she said and pecked his cheek. "How gloss! I've been hoping you'd come in again. Such a sweetie. You know how much I miss you when you're gone. How long has it been since you took me over to Tenta's Fish Fry?"

"A couple quarterns... er maybe more," Schmalch said. He lost track of days sometimes.

That had been quite a night. He'd saved for nearly a month to take her there and spent every last copper before they left. But Ooda was his girlfriend. She liked to do fancy things. He needed to take her places and impress her, or she wouldn't stay interested. It was worth the effort, too—she'd let him sleep over after Tenta's. Warm, dry, and not alone sounded gloss.

"We'll have to do that again soon." Ooda patted his thigh and signaled Garl. "For now, you can buy me a brew."

Garl dropped off the soup with her brew, took more coin, and left.

Schmalch reached for the spoon, but Ooda was faster.

"Garl made some good slop tonight," she said between slurps.

When she paused for a drink, Schmalch snatched the spoon. Ooda might be swish, but he wouldn't be worth twaddle tomorrow without a little food in his belly.

Blobs of fat floated on the oily surface. Something stringy and grey that might have been meat along with beige-ish strips of a chopped root sank to the bottom. Schmalch spooned some into his mouth and widened his eyes in surprise. Garl had used salt and something that tasted kind of like burned onion. It was good—not as good as the orphanage, but pretty gloss for the Barnacle.

When she'd finished half the brew, Ooda stared at him, mouth open, eyes wide. "Are you going to leave any of that for me?"

He gulped in two more mouthfuls and handed her the spoon.

Ooda clicked her tongue at him and resumed eating, pausing only when Schmalch scratched his arm. Then, she put down the spoon and leaned away from him.

"You haven't got scabies again, do you?" she asked.

He rolled up his sleeve and looked at the spot he'd been scratching. Finding no sign of the burrowing mites, he offered her his arm.

"See, all good," Schmalch said.

Ooda inspected the spot before finishing both the soup and her brew and signaling Garl for another round. Schmalch watched more of his coin vanish.

"Did you hear," she asked him, "Yemenie is working evening stage next quartern? She keeps them drinking—but getting the best shift? Emonon is all lathered and claiming Garl's boxing Yemenie's compass. It was only two months back Emonon finished having that tail grown, and now he's replacing her with an oversized pair of bubs?"

Schmalch liked Yemenie well enough. She and Frabo played sleebach with him sometimes. Emonon didn't really seem to notice he existed, but then she was that way with anyone who didn't tip. Schmalch didn't care who got the evening stage. His favorite act was the twins who did the rhythmic thing around midday. They weren't good dancers, but their jerky movements made him chuckle. Those guys never noticed him either.

"Do you think I should get zoet parlor bubs?" Ooda squeezed hers up at Schmalch.

"No, yours are really gloss Ooda." Schmalch couldn't imagine the amount of coin it took for zoetic enhancements or why anyone would pay for a tail, webbed fingers, or weird colored eyes and hair. He was lucky when he had enough coppers to eat and enjoy a few brews at the end of the day.

"Grat, Schmalch, but they could do with a little plump." Ooda looked into the air a beat and changed the subject. "Did you hear about Mimble? She's pregnant again!"

Schmalch nodded and sipped his drink. He had no idea who Mimble was.

In the time it took to blink, Ooda had filled him in on all the staff gossip and ordered another round on his tab. It was expensive to have a girlfriend, but the things she did with her mouth made it really worthwhile.

Schmalch shifted and realized the brew had gone through him.

"I need to fill a pot," he said, slipping off the stool.

Ooda polished off her drink and, already one ahead, signaled for another. "You want one too?" she asked.

Schmalch nodded. He may as well enjoy himself before he was out in the rain again.

During his trudge to the lav, he counted the remaining coppers. He'd already gone through more than half of what he'd picked, and it wasn't yet midnight. If Garl found out how little he had left, Schmalch would be out on his ear well before closing time. He didn't relish the idea of walking to the Upper Rabble in the rain and spending another night under a rowboat at Tendle's Marine.

A tap on his shoulder stopped him before he made it to the toilets.

"Schmalch?" asked a soft voice.

A little shorter and a lot less rigged than Ooda, Plu stood nearby, dingy apron at her waist. She wasn't a Spriggan like Schmalch—Garl hadn't just taken her in after one of the orphanage's graduations—he'd actually *hired* Plu and paid her a nightly wage. He was that way with all his servers and dancers.

Spriggans earned their room and board with drudge work and picking pockets. If anyone got caught, they were gone. Garl couldn't risk customers knowing he was in on the scaling, but he could always grab more filchers

Schmalch had gotten caught. No more working the customers for him. Anytime he owed Garl since then, he was lucky to work it off as the drudge.

Plu moved out of the way of a passing customer and blinked up at Schmalch.

He sighed, wishing he had a nightly wage to look forward to. "Vrasaj, Plu."

"Apologies. I... um... I didn't mean to bother you." She looked at her feet and started to walk away. "It was nothing."

"Wait. I'm just on my way..." he jerked his head toward to lav. "I can wait."

She hesitated before continuing. "I-I know you're... worldly."

"Huh?"

Her face flushed pine and she pointed at the exit. "I mean, I know you know how to live out there."

"Oh." It was his turn to look at his feet. "Yeah."

"No, I mean that's good." She put a hand on his arm, immediately jerking it away. "I need help from someone smart and capable. You were the first person I thought of."

A passer-by bumped into Schmalch, tossing him into Plu. Her face went even darker green.

"I-I-I..." She stepped back, put a hand over her chest, and mumbled to herself before continuing. "I wondered if you could get me a shocker? I'd buy one, but they're so expensive and my rent's due and..."

"Why do you need a shocker?"

She hesitated, scanning the crowd. "There's a new sailor coming in on the *Spinning Compass* every quartern. He..." The color that had faded from her cheeks rose again. "He's been groping me. Then, last night, he waited outside with his fid out and told me there's silver to be had." Plu straightened and glanced toward the bar. "I don't want to insult anyone, but I'm no trull."

Schmalch nodded. He'd passed up more than one proposition even if it meant a warm place to sleep. Why anyone would be obsessed with Plu, though, was beyond him. Her face was scarred up, her nose too flat, and she was so skinny, especially for someone with a steady wage.

"Can't you borrow a knife from here?" he asked.

"Oh, no. I don't want to kill the guy, and you know what Garl would do if I stabbed a customer."

Schmalch grunted in agreement. Garl would toss her to the Corps if he didn't toss her body into the harbor.

"Not right now, Plu," he said, "but I can ask around."

"That'd be great, Schmalch. That'd be great." She smiled bigger than he'd seen before. "I won't bother you anymore."

"What did mousy little Plu want?" Ooda asked when Schmalch returned from the lav.

Another man was sitting in his seat, smirking down at Schmalch like he belonged there. He even took a gulp of Schmalch's fresh brew before getting down from the stool. The tattoo on his arm said *The Portentous Storm*. Schmalch knew that crew. They weren't very nice.

The sailor stared hard at Schmalch and said, "C'mon, Ooda, let's go someplace without pests."

Schmalch scoffed and climbed up on his stool.

"Maybe next time we can go to Tenta's." Ooda finished her brew and kissed Schmalch on the cheek. "You've almost filled the hold."

She slid off the stool and handed her fuzzy pink coat to the sailor, who slipped a little purse in its pocket before helping her into the sleeves.

Schmalch watched numbly as they crossed the room, arm-in-arm. He wasn't sure what he'd done wrong. At least he wouldn't have to share his last few coppers.

Before the door could close on Ooda and her friend, Sigrin Malpockey appeared. Schmalch scrunched down in his seat, trying to hide behind his neighbors, but the chivori women were too bony to provide much cover. Sigrin came in a few steps and looked around, pausing on Schmalch with a smile, before he left again.

A chill ran through Schmalch. Sigrin and his crew would be waiting tonight when he left the Barnacle, he was sure of it. Rain *and* a beating. He took a big gulp and stared glumly into what remained of his drink. Not much to look forward to. Maybe he should give Plu his kris and be done with it.

Skegmubble had given him the little knife when he graduated from the orphanage, telling Schmalch it was lucky. Two nights later Skegmubble was dead. Maybe if he'd still had the kris, he wouldn't have been beaten to death by the Corps. Schmalch was confident he'd die too if he ever gave away the little dagger. Sigrin might take it as payment tonight anyway. With Plu, at least somebody nice would have the kris. Even if she didn't want to kill the guy, it'd be better than nothing.

Schmalch's skin prickled. A few paces away, Garl's eyes slanted his direction. Schmalch's brew was all but gone.

"Where'd your little girlfriend go?" Garl asked, strolling over.

"Ooda left." He tried not to sound too upset about it.

Garl's eyes narrowed at the door. "Alone?"

Schmalch looked at the bar top. "No. She left with a guy. Some sailor for *The Portentous Storm*."

Garl pulled a little pad and marking stick from his pocket and scribbled something down. "Yet she sat here and drank away all your coin. She really knows how to tickle a puka's taint."

"She'll be back. I'm gonna take her to Tenta's again." He wasn't sure why he'd said that. He couldn't afford another drink, let alone two meals.

"You're never gonna get off the street if you don't stop trusting anybody who turns their shine on you. You're like a twitching stray cat. Now," Garl flicked the near-empty mug with a thick finger. "You want another?"

"I'm not quite done with this one yet," Schmalch said. He really wanted one, but he needed the coin he had—and to find a little more—before he walked out past Sigrin.

Garl eyeballed the glass. "Mostly backwash by this point."

"Gimmie a few," Schmalch pleaded. "I'm... I'm about to come into some coin. Promise."

"What? You? Having a payday?"

Schmalch gulped and rolled into the lie. "Yeah, I got a regular job."

"Who'd hire you?"

Schmalch tried to smile. "Well, you did... once."

"And got rid of you too, didn't I?"

"Maybe I could do a few things for you around here to cover another brew? In addition to my other job, I mean."

"I got my needs covered," Garl told Schmalch, scanning the crowd.

"Come on, Garl, those kids don't know how to wash a window like I do."

Garl snorted. "Looks like they've been washed with your dirty chute when you're done with them." He grinned.

Schmalch put on his friendliest smile. "Or I could do a little crowd work for you. I've gotten better, and it's been… it's been nearly three years since… you know, since what happened. They've all forgotten. I'm a customer now." He raised his drink. "Just like them."

Garl shook his head. "Caught's caught. You're out."

"C'mon, Garl. No one else'll remember. I do good work, right?"

Garl shook his head and jerked a thumb toward the door.

Schmalch's pleas leaked out as a whine.

"Cut that noise out or I'll cut it outta you."

Someone down the bar whistled, and Garl signaled back.

"You better be gone or ready to buy a fresh one when I come back." He snorted and spit in the mug. "Drink up, little man."

Schmalch looked at the glossy glob then up at the bartender's ruddy, smirking face and took the tiniest of sips. "See? I'm working on it."

With a final glare, Garl left.

Schmalch stared into his mug. Ruined.

After a while, the chattering chivori women sitting next to him moved on, which was gloss. Not only had they kept their bags on the bar—out of his reach—but they didn't get drunk enough to be careless.

Schmalch was pleased when a pair of karju claimed the seats—much better for hiding behind. Like most of their species, both were big, but the man looked like he could drive Schmalch into the ground with one good thump. He had short brown hair, mostly hidden by a knit watch cap, and what little of his face wasn't covered by beard looked as sun-hardened as any sailor's. The rest of him was so hairy, curls poked out of his collar and sleeves like moss between cobbles. A single hair stuck out of the snoot at the bridge of his nose—the gross little flap that hid whatever it was that made their species so sensitive to smells. He wondered if it tickled. Hair amazed Schmalch—he couldn't imagine living with something like that growing from weird spots on his body.

This woman's hair was longer and lighter than the man's. The tip of her nose was rounder, its bridge wider. Like all karju, their eyes were weirdly small and close together on the fronts of their heads—how did they ever know what was going on beside them? Maybe they could smell it instead. That must be weird.

While the woman flicked the rain from her shoulders, the man stroked sparkly droplets from his beard and pointed to the stool beside Schmalch.

"Sit there," he told her.

Her jacket lifted as she sat down, giving Schmalch a view of the belt purse riding her tailbone. It hung there like ripe fruit, fancier than the drawstring bag he'd plucked earlier. This one attached with a beltloop almost as wide as the purse itself and closed with a buckle.

Schmalch licked his lips. He imagined the purse full of silver, sitting there, waiting for him to take it. Enough coin to keep him at the Barnacle for the rest of the night, tomorrow as well, the whole quartern, possibly the whole month. His mouth watered, thinking of all the things he could buy—a meal as big as he was, a shocker for Plu, a night at Tenta's for Ooda.

Getting to it would be a trick, though.

"Brew for her," the man said when Garl arrived. "Khuit for me."

His voice was a low rumble, the words bitten off like he was angry at them. Schmalch recognized the Imtnor accent from his short time working the docks. It was really bad to be caught scaling down there. He'd once seen a group of dockers hang a thief from a cargo hook in his chest.

"You sure you don't just want a brew?" Garl asked. He hated when people ordered anything else because of something called *low margin*. "Khuit'll cost you. Haven't seen a fresh crate since autumn."

The man stared until Garl left with a shrug and a grumble. Schmalch tried not to giggle.

"Really, Rothis," the woman said. Her voice was soft and quick with the same harsh accent. "*This* is the great place you promised me? It's a... a *sty*. The way you were going on, I thought we'd have a waiter—or at least a table."

Schmalch considered her purse. His kris wouldn't cut through such a thick beltloop without sawing. Even if the woman didn't notice him working—which she almost certainly would—she could flinch or sneeze or something, and he might accidentally stab her. He did *not* want to get thrown in the Bag, and stabbing certainly meant a trip to jail.

"Cork it, Tig," snapped the man—apparently Rothis. "You know why we're here. You wanna go back to your old berry picker with the floppy fid?"

Unbuckle and empty was Schmalch's best option, but he'd have to be gentle. He looked around. No one was playing darts nearby, most everyone in the main room was busy with their own stuff, and the woman's body blocked him from the rest of the bar. Once Garl had dropped off their drinks, the fruit jar would hide Schmalch from his view.

"I left that *old berry picker* because you told me pretty stories about adventure and romance while you were sticking your thumb up my—"

"I said cork it." Rothis pointed at her. "This isn't the place."

Patience pays was a motto the elders had made the kids repeat over and over. He was learning. Right now, all he had to do was wait for Garl to drop off their drinks and avoid being kicked out when he did.

Tig made a *hmpf* sound, and both were quiet until Garl arrived. When he collected their coin, his sour expression and departing snort told Schmalch he wouldn't be back to this end of the bar anytime soon. Though, before leaving, he was sure to jab a threatening finger in Schmalch's direction.

"Sweet Mother Jajal," the woman swore after taking a sniff, "this is barely brew. Made with used socks or something. Trade me. I didn't want this to begin with."

The man downed the khuit in one quick gulp and smiled, teeth like a bright bird in the nest of his beard. He whistled at Garl, signaling for two khuits. Garl gave Rothis his *I'll get to it when I get to it* scowl.

"How did you already manage to gam off the bartender?" Tig asked, pushing her mug away.

Schmalch stared at the ruined brew warning in his mug. He couldn't nurse it much longer. Garl'd be ready to toss him out when he returned with those khuits.

Schmalch rubbed his palms against his still-damp trousers. He wasn't going to find a better opportunity. Slowly, he eased the leather strap out of the first side of the buckle's frame. Tig didn't notice. The prong would be the tricky part, though. If anything was going to draw her notice, it would be the pressure necessary to remove it from the notch.

Schmalch held his breath and drew back the strap.

Rothis' tone softened, "Look Tigania, we do this one little job, and I can get us into the mercenary union. The Abog have to take me with a local reference, right?"

"Sure. I suppose," she said.

"A few jobs here, we'll make enough for passage to Ukur—as passengers instead'a drudges."

"Imt's eyes, don't start on about Ukur again." She sounded tired.

Tig shifted, and for a heartbeat, Schmalch knew he'd been caught. But she was just adjusting—the Barnacle's stools weren't as accommodating for her size as they were for his.

"I wish to Imt you'd never met that Estoan." She sighed.

Slowly, Schmalch let out the breath, and eased the strap through the other half of the frame. Giddy with anticipation, he lifted the flap. Instead of coins, he found a zipper. His excitement deflated.

"No one owns the land there. No spoiled toffs owning everything and telling the working folk how it has to be." Rothis was excited. "It belongs to everyone who works it. We can run our own herd."

Schmalch leaned back and considered the zipper. This close to her body, the woman would feel every tooth release unless he moved so slowly that she'd be ready to leave before he finished opening the purse. His alternative was to fake a tipple, bump into her, and unzip the thing in one smooth stroke. Beg forgiveness afterward. He'd have to be smooth, not fall off the stool. That would draw Garl's attention. Schmalch searched his mind for another tactic but found none.

"I've already played the farmer's wife," Tig said. "Do you think I want to be a herdsman's woman?"

Mumbling a quick appeal to Spriggan, Schmalch grabbed his mug and pitched forward, sloshing the rest of his ruined brew on her jacket with one hand, the other unzipping the purse. He managed to nick two coins before slumping back onto his stool.

Tig whirled on him. Her mouth was pressed in a thin, angry line. "What in the depths are you doing, puka?"

Schmalch waved his empty mug. "Apologies. Maybe I've had too many." He smiled drunkenly and winked. "Or not enough."

"Now, look at this," she showed Rothis her wet jacket. "Is your new minikin friend going to get me one made of made of rat fur to replace it? I hate this city."

Rothis rolled his eyes.

"You," she turned on Schmalch, "don't touch me again."

Schmalch gave her a somber tippler's nod, relaxing only when she'd returned to her conversation.

He eyed the unzipped purse. Plenty of copper waited inside, but he saw silver too. The thought of a pocketful of Callas made moths flutter in his chest. He slipped his fingers in, pinched coins, and had half-removed them when Tig shifted again. The overfull purse jiggled, knocking the coins from his hand. On instinct, Schmalch lunged for them, catching everything but throwing himself off balance. For a heartbeat, he wobbled on the stool's edge, hands groping for something—other than Tig—to grab onto. But he fell, banging into her on the way down, jostling a shower of copper and silver to the floor.

Schmalch landed face-down, the coins pattering on his back like hail. He got to his knees and scrambled to grab them all, certain he could snatch them and run.

"Again?" The woman stood, more coins tumbling out. "What is wrong with you?"

"Enough of this plop, puka," the man said. He grabbed Schmalch by the arm and lifted him off the floor. "Check your purse, Tig. The little douse's been trying to rob you."

"Let go," Schmalch said. His arm felt like it was going to come off. "It hurts."

The man pulled a polished dagger from inside his coat. "It's gonna hurt more when I open your belly."

Garl grabbed his club and started down the bar toward them. "Hey! If you're going to knife him, do it outside!"

Rothis snorted and stuck his dagger into the bar top, still dangling Schmalch. "No need, barkeep. I'm just holding him until the law comes."

Schmalch felt panic well inside. The law meant the Corps and the Corps meant he'd be dead or in one of the Bag's cells before morning. A whine forced its way up from his lungs and through his tightening throat.

"What's that sound he's making?" Rothis asked Tig.

"I don't know, but it's awful," she said, kneeling to pick up her coins.

Schmalch wriggled, hoping to slide free—or maybe his arm

would tear off. He was trying not to panic—when he did, sometimes he couldn't remember what happened next—but the pain was making it tough.

His shoulder popped, agony burst bright, and Schmalch screamed, "Don't give me to the Corps!"

Garl slammed his club on the bar by Rothis' empty glass. "Enough! Take it outside or the Corps'll be your problem too."

Rothis dropped Schmalch and raised his hands. "My fault. I guess the Haven's easier on thieves than we are back home."

"Don't let them take me to the Bag," Schmalch begged as his shoulder snapped back into place. The relief felt almost as good something Ooda would do. "I'll give the coins back. I only wanted another brew or two so Garl won't put me out in the rain."

"What'll you do for me if I don't call them?" Rothis asked.

"Anything, just don't let the Corps take me." Schmalch's hand had gone numb. His shoulder throbbed.

Rothis stared at Schmalch for a long moment. "You'd really do *anything*?"

Schmalch nodded.

Rothis glanced at Garl, who nodded. "Never seen him say no when coin or his hide are concerned."

"Three khuits," Rothis told Garl, "on Tig."

She made a protest noise as she got back onto her stool, but he silenced her with a finger.

"Give Tig anything you managed to pocket," Rothis said, stashing his dagger.

Grudgingly, Schmalch returned a fistful of coins he'd grabbed, holding back a few in case he ran into Sigrin on the way out. Tig would probably figure they'd rolled away in the commotion.

While Garl collected the fresh round, Rothis dragged his stool closer and sat, leather pants creaking like a spooky door. "As it happens, we could use a puka with light fingers. Tig didn't notice you working that swish pouch until I did. If you're as light on your feet, we could use you. Interested in making some silver?"

"What would I have to do?" Schmalch rubbed his shoulder. It wasn't the first time he'd been held like that. It would hurt for a few days, but the pain would go away.

"Nothing harder than Tig's purse."

Schmalch considered. That was a skint description, but he needed coin. He'd gone into his last job for Rift with no information—she had a reputation, a scary one, but she always paid. He wished she ran a crew. Rothis and Tig were strangers, new to the Haven. They'd probably get him thrown in the Bag if he didn't do this job.

Schmalch looked at Tig, who smiled. She was missing a tooth on one side.

"I'll do it," he said.

"I thought you might." Rothis grinned behind his beard. "Meet us at midday tomorrow in Marthoth Air & Sea Warehouse 4. You know where that is, right?"

Schmalch nodded. He'd worked that part of the Upper Rabble in his younger days. Marthoth Air & Sea docks and warehouses were far past Pukatown at the islet's tip—a grey fleet of sheet metal buildings marked with the company's big red logo. Schmalch was a little hazy on where that specific warehouse was, but he was confident he could figure it out.

Garl dropped off the drinks. Tig paid him without protest.

"Right, then we'll see you tomorrow at midday," Rothis said.

He stood and tapped Tig on the shoulder. She headed for the door without a word.

Schmalch stared—they were leaving their drinks untouched.

Rothis pointed a thick finger at him. "Don't be late. Our boss won't like it, and you do not want to be on the wrong end of that."

"I won't." Schmalch's eyes drifted back to the abandoned drinks. "Can I have those?"

He woke the next morning to the screeching of bickering gulls. Missus Tendle had put out breakfast scraps again, and as usual, the birds were fighting over the meal. Schmalch cursed himself—if he hadn't slept so late, he could have had first pickings instead of the scavengers. He'd swiped plenty of meals from the gulls over the years, even survived a couple attacks by the largest among them. He considered ducking into the squabbling gullery to grab some for himself but decided against it. He needed his fingers uninjured if he was going to do this job with Rothis and Tig. Maybe he could get on their boss' crew.

It had been a long, rainy stumble up to the Runoff last night, but at least he'd slept dry—and the spot put him closer to Marthoth's warehouses than sleeping under the Barnacle's awning. The sun was one-hand high when Schmalch rolled out from under the rowboat, wincing when his shoulder bumped its gunnel, sore from the dangling Rothis had given him. The drinks they'd left had made up for the abuse, keeping Schmalch at the bar till closing without spending another copper. When he left, Schmalch even managed to dodge Sigrin and his goons. What started as a scruddy night had turned out pretty gloss.

His belly rumbled and Schmalch sniffed the air. Only dank wood, dead stuff, and seawater, but then it was unlikely he'd find a food cart in a floater neighborhood. Schmalch made his way through the Runoff's ever-changing walkways—a buoyed dock here, a gangway there—to the shore, where Bay Run followed the coast up to Marthoth's warehouses. Not whiff or a glimpse of a food cart. If he was lucky, Schmalch might find a street vendor on his way to the warehouse. Or—thanks to last night's coin—he could make a side trip a few blocks into Pukatown, where his favorite pastry shop was. If he did that, he'd need to scutter to make sure he was on time. It'd be better to get there early, he told himself, but with a painful gurgle, his stomach made the decision.

Schmalch scampered down Pukatown's streets, morning aromas of breads, baked sweet roots, and smoked fish greeting him. There were a lot of breakfast choices on the way, but Itnee's Pastries was his favorite. He'd found them after visiting Ooda's cuddy the first time, and their heta buns were as good as anything served in those swish Big Island restaurants. Plus, they were the cheapest Schmalch had found on the Upper *or* Lower Rabble. He gobbled the first bun before he left the bakery, taking his time on the second so he'd have something to enjoy on his walk to Warehouse 4.

Ooda's windows were open when he passed. He wondered how her night had been. Maybe after he did whatever this was for Rothis, he'd be able to afford to take her to Tenta's again.

"Schmalch!" Ooda's voice sang out.

He looked around but didn't see her.

"Up here. Look up."

Ooda leaned out of her third-story window, light purple bathrobe draped over her shoulders. It looked really soft and fell open in the front in a way Schmalch enjoyed. The cosmetic was gone from her face.

"Did you bring any for me?" she hollered down to him.

"Huh?" he said through a mouthful.

"Buns. Did you bring any for me?"

Schmalch shook his head.

Her brow furrowed. "I'm hurt you didn't think of me."

"I didn't think you were awake. And I have to be at the north tip by midday."

"There's still plenty of time." She flicked a hand. "You can go back and buy me a half-dozen, can't you?"

"I really can't be late."

Ooda stuck out her lip and looked sad.

Schmalch wanted to buy her buns to make her happy. "All right, but I'm kinda skint."

"Fine," she said like she was angry. "Wait there."

Schmalch had finished the second bun by the time Ooda burst from the front door, still in her bathrobe. She was so pretty.

"Here." Ooda pressed some coppers in his palm and handed him a shopping basket. "Six buns and a small tin of loose tea—that kind with black leaves and pink flowers."

"Black leaves and pink flowers."

"Right." She kissed him on the cheek. "Come upstairs and knock when you have it."

Schmalch went back to the bakery, flummoxed when Miss Itnee told him there were three kinds of tea with black leaves and pink flowers. She said a lot of things about the differences so quickly that he couldn't interrupt. When she finally let him explain who it was for, Miss Itnee knew exactly which kind to pick.

Schmalch was feeling like a good boyfriend when he knocked on Ooda's door. She answered quickly, blocking the opening with her body, robe still pleasantly open in front.

"That was fast," she said, snatching the basket. "I'd invite you in, but I have company. You know how it is."

"It's, er, fine. I mean, I have to make the meet for that job."

"A job, I like to hear that." She tapped the tip of his nose. "Maybe we'll visit the Fish Fry sooner than I thought."

His face went warm. "Yeah. I don't know how mu—"

"Hey Ooda," a man's voice called from inside. "Where do you keep your towels?"

"Hold on," she replied. "We'll talk about the Fish Fry when your job's over, Schmalch."

He nodded, trying to ignore the sailor's muttered complaints. Schmalch didn't like it that Ooda had a lot of boyfriends, but until he was rich enough to be her only boyfriend, he'd live with it.

"Grat for the buns," She said and shut the door.

Feeling less like a good boyfriend, he made his way back to Bay Run and followed it until he spotted the Marthoth Air & Sea logo.

The further north he went, the more buildings featured the big red splotch.

Nobody was waiting outside for him at Warehouse 4, so Schmalch went inside. What looked like three stories of building turned out to be a giant room filled with livestock pens. It stank. More piglets than he could count milled around inside the nearest one. A couple rhochrots towered over them—counting or herding or feeding, Schmalch couldn't tell. They looked comical, so huge that the pigs scrambled around beneath them. With four thick legs and feet made more for crushing than caution, Schmalch was impressed neither of the rhochrots accidentally squashed a piglet or two with every step.

In the aisles and other pens, a handful of people were doing things that were probably their jobs. Rothis and Tig weren't among them. Schmalch's throat tightened. They hadn't said where to go once he was inside. He was lost. He wasn't going to get the job. Another chance of getting on a crew ruined.

"Who're you?" A big-bellied karju in stained coveralls walked up.

"I'm—uh—I'm looking for Rothis."

The man stared.

"Or Tig?"

"I don't know who those people are."

"I'm supposed to meet them," Schmalch said. "Marthoth Air & Sea Warehouse 4."

He shook his head and pointed. "You want the next one. That way."

Schmalch ran there, hoping he wasn't too late.

Rothis stood outside. Between the hat and beard, it was tough to gauge his expression, but his tone was annoyed.

"Where've you been?" he asked. "It's practically aftermid."

"I, um, I got lost," Schmalch said. "The buildings look the same."

"No fuge, that's why they have numbers." Rothis opened the door and motioned for Schmalch to follow him inside.

Instead of livestock pens, this warehouse was filled with shelves so tall they probably connected to the ceiling. A swarm of people fluttered around, moving boxes, barrels, and crates on and off the shelves using roll-around metal carts and all sorts of complicated-looking equipment Schmalch couldn't have used on a bet. Zoet-muscled ponies pulled loaded platforms—tenders at the rear prodding them on—while others dragged long ropes attached to complicated series of pullies.

Despite being certain the towering shelves would collapse and crush him, Schmalch followed Rothis into the gap between two rows, jogging to stay in his wake. Busy employees moved around Rothis like he wasn't even there. No one spoke or even made eye contact, they just avoided him like minnows around a reef. Schmalch only knew one other person who could do that.

He was starting to sweat by the time they reached a bright yellow staircase that led to a windowed, white box atop a web of bright yellow beams. It looked like someone was storing their apartment inside the warehouse.

Schmalch wiped his forehead on the tail of his shirt and followed Rothis up the steps. A bald karju man waited at the top, his face pattern-scarred, the ridges tattooed dark red. A shocker hung at one hip, fighting knife at his other. He opened the door and Rothis marched inside. Schmalch gave the guard a wide berth as he entered, unnerved when the bald man followed him through.

Inside, the white box was mostly empty, as if someone had just moved in. A couple roll-around carts like the ones on the warehouse floor sat to one side of the door, a jumble of crates stacked on top, marked with the red splotch of Marthoth Air & Sea.

Rothis stepped to the side and nudged Schmalch toward a big metal desk, where a pale woman with dark brown curls was dwarfed by her high-backed chair. She was the same size, had the same sharp nose, the same angry green eyes as the man who stood behind her—Sigrin Malpockey.

Schmalch went cold. This was a trap. Sigrin had planned it, punishment for fouling the catnapping. Any moment now, his goons would burst out the other door and beat Schmalch senseless, maybe even kill him.

He wheeled to run and banged into Rothis' thighs, falling back on his ass, stunned.

"What in the depths was that about?" Rothis picked Schmalch up by his sore arm, holding him out like a carnival prize.

Schmalch yelped, skin crawling at Sigrin's cackling response.

"Shut it, Siggy," the woman snapped. "And put the puka down, Rothis, you tit. He can't do what we need him to do with a dislocated shoulder."

"I was just trying to help," Rothis grumbled, releasing Schmalch.

He rubbed his shoulder and considered escape, but the bald man had closed the door and moved in front of it. Schmalch was trapped.

"Well, you weren't," the woman said. "You were breaking our thief. This *is* him, right?"

Schmalch's panic started to clear. He wasn't sure what was going on, but no one was beating him. That was good.

"Yep," Rothis said, "the one I was telling you about. Schmaltz."

"Schmalch." Tig corrected. Schmalch hadn't noticed her standing by the windows.

"Right." The woman's eyes shifted to Schmalch. "Tig says you almost took her purse last night. Rothis says you're looking for work."

Schmalch kept massaging his shoulder and nodded. Best to keep silent when he didn't know the rub.

"Quiet," she said. "I like that. I have a job for a thief like you."

Something inside Schmalch warmed. He liked being called *thief* a whole lot more than *gutter baby*.

"Are you interested in working for me?"

Schmalch paused. This still felt like a trap. He'd fouled the last job he'd done for Sigrin, still owed him ever-increasing amounts of coin, so why was his sister being so nice? Still, being on a crew would be better than working alone, even if he did have to put up with Sigrin's snark.

"Uh huh," Schmalch said.

"Did Rothis tell you who I am?"

"Uh-uh."

"So, he's not a complete dunder. I'm Mallow Malpockey." She poked a thumb behind her. "I'm told you already know this pile of birdlime, right baby brother?"

"Twins, Mallow," Sigrin said.

"Born first is born first." Mallow chuckled.

Schmalch looked from her to Sigrin, who stared sullenly back. They looked alike, but while Sigrin always looked ready to punch someone, Mallow seemed like she'd prefer to bite. Minikin or not, she was clearly nasty enough to boss around people like Rothis and Tig.

"Siggy's whining aside, sit down." She gestured to the chair in front of her desk. "Why'd you try to run?"

"Like you said," Schmalch scratched a spot that wasn't even itchy, "I know Sigrin."

"How about that, Jeho?" Mallow said to the scary door guard, "Baby brother actually has someone afraid of him." She returned to Schmalch. "You know what Siggy does for coin?"

"He runs the Grey Boots," Schmalch said.

Mallow guffawed, "Runs the Grey Boots? I run the Grey Boots. The only thing Siggy runs are errands. Like last night, I sent him to locate you. I've heard about you, Schmalch, one of the best thieves in the Rabbles." Mallow snapped her fingers. "Siggy, bring out the drink cart. Remember ice this time."

Sigrin held Schmalch's gaze.

"*Now*, baby brother."

With an angry mumble, Sigrin left through a door at the back of the room.

"You see, Schmalch, he's not a thief, he's a drudge—and not a particularly good one." Mallow leaned back in her seat. "He's been nearly useless since he slid out of dear old mom behind me. She should've kept her legs crossed and made the world better."

Schmalch stifled a giggle.

The door opened and Sigrin wheeled in a little silver cart loaded with glasses, colorful bottles, and a bright-red bucket. He looked funny, like a snooty waiter at a fancy Big Island restaurant. Schmalch snorted. Sigrin scowled.

"Four khuits," Mallow said, smiling in a way that reminded Schmalch of an angry cat. "Ice for me."

"You sure, Mallow?" Sigrin asked. "You're not gonna call it swill and dump it on the floor again?"

Mallow rolled her eyes. "Just pour the drinks."

Sigrin dumped ice into one glass and poured, the thick yellow liquid clinging to the chilled glass like skin. He handed it to his sister and poured three more without ice, serving Rothis and Tig before offering a glass to Schmalch, who could only stare. Being served by Sigrin Malpockey seemed like a dream had after too much of Garl's brew.

When he tried to take the khuit, Sigrin held tight.

"You still owe me *two* Callas, puka, and I better see payment when you finish this job. Provided you don't foul this one too." His sneer shifted to nasty smile. "If you live through it."

Schmalch swallowed. He'd had no idea death was a possibility.

"Ignore him, Schmalch," Mallow said. "He's not up for a job as big as this."

Sigrin snorted.

Mallow downed her khuit and tossed the ice cubes on the floor. "Disgusting. Clean that up and pour me another without ice."

Sigrin jabbed a finger at Schmalch. "Two Callas." He grabbed a towel from the cart and started picking up ice.

Schmalch sipped his khuit, strong and smelling a little like the stuff Garl used to wash windows. Still, it was free.

"The job's simple," Mallow said. "Rothis and Tig are too noticeable. We need someone of a reasonable size to slip in, retrieve the boodle and get back out. Should anything happen, they'll be there to watch out for you. That's it. Simple, right?"

"Simple. Yeah," Schmalch agreed. Sigrin had just been trying to scare him. Even if something did go wrong, being with two burly karju as nasty as Rothis and Tig would keep him safe.

"We're waiting on the last bit of gen for the plan. Come back same time tomorrow so Rothis and Tig can walk you through details." Mallow flipped a hand at him.

"Time to go," Rothis said.

"How, uh, much does the job pay?" Schmalch asked.

Mallow shrugged. "How does three Callas sound?"

"It sounds gloss!" That kind of silver would keep Schmalch on his stool at the Barnacle for a full quartern—half that if Ooda found out. Of course, Sigrin would know and want two of them. Maybe Schmalch could dodge him for another quartern or two.

The evening had been mostly dry, which was good because Schmalch didn't have enough coin to stay at the Barnacle. He'd headed north to Tendle's Marine to sleep under a boat again—just in case the spring rain reappeared.

He sat tucked between two upturned dinghies, the sea on one side, shadows to the other. His stomach rumbled, but a meal would have to wait until Missus Tendle put out her breakfast scraps in the morning. He promised himself he'd wake up early this time and be ready when she set them out. If he was quick, he could grab them before the gulls noticed. Schmalch was a good thief—at least when stealing from the birds.

He was a little nervous about the job for Mallow, a little surprised she'd take him on after the way things had gone with Sigrin. She seemed as mean as her brother, but smarter and nastier. Maybe Sigrin didn't tell her Schmalch had botched the last job. Maybe he was trying to trick her for some reason. Either way, she'd given Schmalch a paying job. Best not to overthink a gift, as Elder Tamerlyyn used to say. If Mallow liked his work, it would mean being part of a crew—at least he hoped so. The best way to stay fed on Dockhaven was to be on a crew. It meant regular work, reliable coin, backup, and someone else finding marks and making plans instead of doing it all himself.

Schmalch wasn't going to flub this job. The catnapping had gone sideways because he was impatient, a little tippled, and hadn't thought to close the apartment door once he was inside. The Corps had nearly grabbed the whole crew while they were chasing the escaped cat down Central Row. He was going to stay sharp for this job, save the drinking for celebrating afterward.

Working with a crew was different from working on his own. Schmalch knew he'd improve with practice, like back when he'd struggled learning to pick pockets. He had to live through the frustration and taunts whenever he failed now, just like back then. But if after every mistake, he remembered not to repeat it, eventually he'd know what to do so easily, he'd be as good as any Thung Toh operative.

He'd like that—sneaking around, taking what he wanted, being better at it than most anyone else. He'd watched under the arms of people paying for the coin-operated flickers at places like the Triangle and Saxelyt's Gatehouse. The Toh stories were thrilling—stealthy, nimble thieves slipping into the most guarded places on the isles, slipping out again unnoticed, boodle in hand. Sometimes, he'd seen bits where the operatives guarded important people or forged art or broke people out of jail—sometimes they even broke bones and slit throats. Schmalch wasn't sure he was cut out for that part, but the sneaking around and taking things seemed perfect.

Did they get to pick their jobs? Or did someone assign them like the elders at the orphanage had assigned chores? Schmalch supposed he could do anything for enough coin—and the flickers were always clear that Thung Toh operatives earned a lot of coin for being so swish.

Something shifted in the shadows beside him and Schmalch jumped so far he almost fell off the dock. A grey and black spotted cat—the one Missus Tendle called Kook—stepped into view, eyeing Schmalch with a mixture of curiosity and fear. She moved close enough to smell his foot, but not close enough to be snatched or stroked.

"Sneaking up on me, huh?" Schmalch whispered to the cat.

She blinked. He'd shared scraps with Kook once. Now she was his friend. If only he could get her to cuddle.

Schmalch leaned forward, slowly reaching for the cat, but the instant his fingers brushed fur, she hissed and darted back into the shadows.

"A daring escape, but don't think you can get away from me that easily. Hand over the gen and I won't have to end you, Professor Kook."

Pressing his back against a rowboat, Schmalch eased along its hull like a Thung Toh operative slipping along a wall, the prize beyond the next turn. At the bow, he whirled around the corner, startling Kook, who leapt on top of the little boat and gave him another hiss.

"I've got you now," he whispered to the cat, raising one hand, finger pointed like a pistol. "I have a contract to close."

She looked at him cockeyed and licked one paw.

"Resisting, eh?" Schmalch edged closer to the cat's perch, finger changed from pistol to knife. "I'll make it quick."

Within a step of Kook, Schmalch lunged, attempting to swipe his knife-finger across her fluffy neck, but instead losing his balance and falling against the boat, sending it rocking into the next one and the next. The cat made a terrible noise and leapt away. The hollow clatter of wood on wood echoed across the quiet bay like a drumroll.

A light came on inside Tendle's. Schmalch dove into the shadows.

The rattling of keys, creak of a door, and someone called out, "Who's there?" A pause. "I have a gun and I'm not afraid to use it. You're not taking my dinghies."

The cat sidled up to Schmalch, head-butting him. *Now* she wanted to cuddle. Schmalch gave her a couple strokes and silently apologized before tossing Kook out from behind the boat. She landed gracefully and glared back at him with a hiss, betrayal on her face. The next time Schmalch got some scraps he'd share them.

"Oh, it's you," Missus Tendle said.

Schmalch's heart skipped. Had she seen him?

"You're lucky I don't really have a gun, you scruffy old kook."

Not him, but the cat. Schmalch relaxed.

The door creaked shut and the light went out. Schmalch gently lifted the gunwale of one rowboat and slid beneath, curling up for sleep. In a moment, Kook joined him.

2085 MEDIBAR 15

The next morning, Schmalch arrived at Warehouse 4 on time but with an empty belly—the gulls had gobbled Missus Tendle's scraps long before he'd opened an eye. He hoped Rothis and Tig would bring breakfast to the meeting, but knew it was a long shot.

Rain had restarted last night, and Schmalch was doused by the time he reached Marthoth's warren of grey warehouses, jogging between them as fast as the slick cobbles allowed. Tig was waiting at the entrance this time. She talked a lot while they walked to Mallow's office.

"Rothis is late," she told him, her hands twitching like baby birds as she talked. "I've come to expect this. He's all lathered when somebody isn't where he wants them, but when he's supposed to be somewhere? Well, we can all stand around and wait while he's off stroking his critter. Typical. How could he do this to me right before this job?"

Schmalch almost asked why she hadn't expected Rothis to be late if this was typical, but Ooda had told him to stay silent when it came to other people's relationships, saying, "You don't know what kind of crazy they've got going in there."

Tig looked over her shoulder. "Everything he promises turns to plop, you catch?"

Schmalch nodded. She was walking fast. He had to run to keep up.

"When I met him, Rothis told me all these stories of romance and adventure. I believed he'd actually done this kind of work before. I'm a gudgeon. My life was good as mistress of the meadery. I had a dodder of a husband, true, but I was lady of the manor—not an actual lady, maybe, but I could've been had the old man spent some time at court. We would have had a title in no time. But me, I fell for a farm hand with a big fid and a tale to tell. I should have known none of it was true." She gestured at the world around her, the surrounding workers ignoring her. "This is hardly the glamourous life of derring-do he promised."

Schmalch wondered what *daring-do* was.

"We barely made it out of Imt Hold aboard the *Damsel's Distress* and—boom—he's fast friends with some Estoan sailor. Next thing I know he wants to explore Ukur, but the *Damsel* isn't going to Ukur. Now I'm stuck on this stinking mound waiting for him to get enough coin together for passage to Guunaat while the little I got for living in that berry patch with the dodder drains away on four-copper meals that aren't worth one." She paused for a breath. "Four coppers! You can get a full spread breakfast in Imt Hold for half that. I hate this city."

As they climbed the stairs to Mallow's office, Tig kept talking about all the awful stuff that had happened to her since she left home. Schmalch felt bad for her, but some of it just made him uncomfortable.

Inside, the room was empty, the Malpockeys and the bald guard nowhere to be seen.

Tig flopped into Mallow's chair and propped her feet on the desk. "Do you know what the worst part's been?" she asked Schmalch.

He shook his head, hoping Rothis would arrive.

"I was more that Estoan's type than he was, you catch? But that's how far I've had to go to get him to stop flogging and start thinking about our future. Of course, this scheme is what he comes up with. I should probably leave him and hop on the next ship back to Imt Hold."

Rothis opened the door.

"Where've you been?" Tig asked. "Even this drudge got here on time today."

"I met a connection at the bathhouse and couldn't be rude. She may have another job for us."

Tig sat up, little eyes narrowing. "I thought you were joining the Abog Union after this one."

"Yeah, I'm going to do that too, but extra coin means getting out of here sooner. I thought that's what you wanted."

Tig threw up her hands.

Rothis joined them at the desk, unfolding a map and spreading it out on top. "We start here," He stabbed a spot with his thick finger. "The supposedly empty lab."

Schmalch joined Tig on the other side of the desk for a better view. He was impressed to find so many drawers with shiny handles. He wanted to know what was in all of them.

The map was of the Big Island, its southeast coast circled. Schmalch knew the neighborhood—mostly trades workshops and warehouses bordered by Temple Row and the creepy old desal plant.

Rothis sat on the corner of the desk, rain-damp leather pants creaking. "It seems Integrated Zoetics is doing some secret research," he said. "Boss says it looks closed from the outside, but they have a team of zoeticists living in the upper stories, working in the lower." He looked at Schmalch. "You catch?"

Schmalch nodded. "You need me to get something from there?"

"Yeah." He pulled out another map, this one hand-drawn by someone who didn't understand maps. Rothis tapped an oblong box on the page. "We'll slip you in through the transom above this door here. It should open wide enough for that head of yours."

"What's a *tran-sum*?" Schmalch asked.

Rothis grunted and shook his head.

"It's one of those windows at the top of a door that opens up like this." Tig put her hands together at an angle. "Imt's eyes, Rothis, remember he's as ignorant as any rube working the fields."

"Um, grat," Schmalch said. "So, will I fall going in?"

"Probably," Rothis said. "Try to catch the lip as you slide through and let yourself down easy. But it'll still be a drop. Once you're in, first thing you need to grab is the keys. The gen says both guards carry rings with all the ones we'd need."

"Guards?"

"Yeah, two guards standard. No animals. Alarm, but we'll take care of that."

"How?"

Rothis' brow wrinkled. "I'll get to it. Just cork your hole and listen."

Schmalch nodded.

"What was I saying?"

"The guards," Tig said.

"Right. Two guards standard at night, which is when we're going in. All the squints should be upstairs by then. You'll need to lift the keys from one of the guards. They patrol in two routes." Rothis traced two paths through the building. "When they're not on patrol, the boss says they're usually in the commissary." He pointed to an uneven square at the back of the building. "When you have the keys, take them to Lab 3." His finger moved to a circled room in the middle of the building. "You'll need one of the keys to get in, two more for the safe."

"What kind?" Schmalch asked. Many safes needed more than keys to open, and Schmalch had no talent for combinations or puzzles.

"Source says it's about my height, painted brown, double doors."

"He means what kind of lock, you tit," Tig said.

"Didn't I tell you to cork it?" Rothis pointed at her, beard quivering, before continuing with an angry growl in his voice. "Two-key lock, one for each door. You can't open it without using both at the same time. You should be able to manage that, right?"

Schmalch nodded.

Rothis pulled out a picture of a black ball with lines crisscrossing its surface. "Find this in the safe and pocket it."

"What is it?" Schmalch asked. "Candy? It looks like a candy."

Rothis rubbed his eyes and pinched his snoot in frustration.

"It's a polymerized microzoet bio-sample case that requires a solvent to unseal," Tig said.

Rothis glared at her.

"What?" Tig asked him. "Do you think he understood a word of that? *You* didn't understand it until the boss explained it to you."

"You fancy, two-copper—" Rothis began.

"Will it hurt me?" Schmalch interrupted.

"Son of dibuc. No, it won't hurt you" Rothis said. "That's what she just said."

Tig snorted. "That *candy*, Schmalch, is a sealed bottle that won't open unless it's given a special bath."

Schmalch considered. "What's in the bottle?"

"Medicine for propulsors. That's all you need to know."

"Now, can you both keep it corked so I can finish?" Rothis pushed the watch cap back on his head and closed his eyes for a moment.

Schmalch had never imagined zoets took medicine like people did. What kind of medicine did propulsors take and how? Zoeticists had designed the big wormy creatures to move ships faster than wind across the sea. Everything that went in one mouth quickly came out the one at the other end, so they couldn't swallow the same kind of medicine Elder Tamerlyyn had given Schmalch. Unless those weren't their mouths. He giggled.

"Do you catch?" Rothis asked through clenched teeth.

Schmalch put on his serious face and nodded. He needed to pay attention to this stuff.

"Once you have the sample container, meet us at the front door—where you started. You'll need another key for that."

"But you'll take care of the alarm."

"Of course. That's what we'll be doing while you're grabbing the sample."

"How?"

"Imt's eyes. We'll cut the line from the cap-array, right? The gen tells us where it is and how to do it. Anything else, your lordship?"

Schmalch scratched his chin. Steal the keys, steal the sample, open the front door. Simple enough. He hoped it would stop raining by then. It was hard to be sneaky when his shoes squelched.

"Nope," Schmalch said.

"Good. Meet us here tomorrow at dusk and we'll take the Pipe up to the Big Island."

"It'd be faster to ride the tram and come up the south coast,"

Schmalch said.

Rothis stared at him for a moment. "How much does that cost?"

"A copper. Each."

"Fine, we'll take the tram."

"Can we meet at the station?"

Rothis' teeth showed briefly through the net of his mustache. "Fine, we'll meet at the tram station, which is…?"

Schmalch chuckled. Everyone who'd spent two days in Dockhaven knew where the tram stations were.

"It's by the Bitter Barnacle—where we met. Remember?" He smiled. When Rothis didn't smile back, Schmalch leaned over the desk and pointed to the Big Island map. "It goes to here. Then we turn just before the Caba Club, and Temple Row goes all the way to High Road."

For a moment Schmalch thought Rothis might yell. Instead he nodded. "Fine. It's as good as anything."

Tig snorted.

"We'll meet at the tram at nightfall." Rothis tapped the station on the map. "If you need us before then, we're at the Belvedor Inn."

"In the meantime, you should visit the bathhouses," Tig said, finger over her snoot. "You won't be able to sneak up on anything with a pong like that. And fresh clothes. I don't think that smell will wash out of fabric."

"I don't have any coin," Schmalch said.

"Fine," Rothis huffed. "Tig, hand me that purse the boss gave you."

She frowned but passed a drawstring bag to him.

For a moment, Schmalch tingled all over, picturing the Callas that might be inside. Then Rothis picked out all the silver.

"Here," he gave the purse to Schmalch and turned to leave. "Wash up and buy new duds."

"Hey!" Tig protested. "How am I supposed to pay for our room?"

Rothis tossed two Callas on the desk and left.

Schmalch liked the Pukatown bath houses the best. All white-tiled and steamy, they had lots of tubs instead of just a couple of big pools that everyone had to share. Though a few pukas could fit into one, Schmalch usually managed to bathe alone if he didn't know anyone or feel like talking. Best of all were the private dressing stalls and free, clean towels big enough to wrap yourself—which meant less awkward nakedness around strangers. Most of the other Rabble bath houses didn't give anyone a towel until they came out of the water. He hated walking around with his fid and jugglers out.

First shifters were at work and the place was largely empty, a handful of pukas lingering in warm baths, a couple karju soaking in the deep pools toward the rear.

Schmalch snagged a towel, paid the attendant an extra copper for a nub of bland-smelling soap, and made his way to the stalls. He picked the first empty one he found, stripped down, and covered as much of his body as possible with the towel before exiting, jangling purse tight in his fist. No way he was leaving that in the stall for someone to scale.

The showers were warm, but not so hot as Elder Sriree had used at the orphanage. He scrubbed fast and with much splashing, spraying himself completely to rinse before resuming the towel. He sniffed at all the stinky places he could reach and checked himself in a mirror on his way to the tubs. His cheeks were piney, no streaks of food, muck, or whatever else.

Though it was quiet, every pool had someone in it. A soak would have been nice, but he wasn't feeling like being talked at by a naked stranger.

Now he just had to find clean clothes.

He was considering which castoff shop would be cheapest when someone hollered, "Schmalch!"

He looked around and spotted Dinnlit waving at him from a steaming pool in the far corner. Dinnlit was a sliphand, though all he would admit to being was "a shopkeeper without a shop." They'd met a year or so after Schmalch graduated from the orphanage, and Schmalch had unloaded dosh to him a few times. Dinnlit might be able to locate a cheap shocker for Plu.

Schmalch adjusted his towel to hide the now-damp purse and walked over to Dinnlit's sunken pool. Lighter green than Schmalch, his skin was starting to wrinkle. He sat with arms spread, smiling vaguely.

"Erm… Vrasaj, Dinnlit?"

The smile blossomed. "It's been a while, Schmalch. Anything to sell?"

"No, no, not today. But… I am looking to buy."

"Excellent. Join me." He patted the water.

Schmalch shifted uncomfortably. Naked in a small pool of water with someone else—it was like the early days at the orphanage when they washed the young ones all together.

"Grat, but I'm in a rush," Schmalch said. "I just wondered if you had a shocker to sell. Not the killing kind, just enough charge to knock a guy out."

Dinnlit frowned thoughtfully. "Had one last quartern, but that sold. I'll put a net out. Check back in a couple days."

"Right. Grat."

"While I'm doing that for you, keep an eye out for any interesting daggers for me. I have a friend who collects different sorts from around the islands."

"Daggers, sure."

"Enjoy the day." The sliphand leaned back, put a steaming cloth over his eyes, and waved Schmalch away.

Schmalch hurried back to his dressing stall. When he pulled back the curtain, he smelled the pong Tig had been talking about coming off his clothes. He didn't even want to put them back on or he'd have to go through this whole washing thing again. But he couldn't leave naked.

The curtain of the neighboring stall fluttered, and a plump man stepped out, towel around his waist. Before the curtain could settle, Schmalch checked if the attendant was looking and slipped in. The man's clothes were nice enough, comfortable, and only a little loose, easily managed by tightening the belt. The jacket was rusty, sun-faded burlap, still scratchy and unpleasant despite use. When he opened it, though, the lining was soft—and it went all the way up to the collar. The deep pockets were a bonus—less chance of things bouncing out. The shoes didn't fit, so Schmalch reached under to snag his old ones and hurried out before his trick was discovered.

Outside, the rain had stopped and the sun was breaking through the clouds, still a hand's width above the city's jumbled horizon. Keeping an eye behind him, he eased away from the front of the building and ducked into the first empty alley.

He was clean. He had new clothes. And he still had a purse-full of coppers—even if it was soaking a damp spot into his new jacket—enough to take Ooda to the Fish Fry *and* eat tomorrow, though he'd be sure to hide the breakfast coins in his shoe.

Mumbling gratitude to Tokimer, Schmalch scampered Ooda's way. He guessed she'd be home, getting ready for a night at the Barnacle—and he was correct. She answered the door with a wary squint, relaxing when she saw him. Her cosmetic was in place—red again tonight—but she hadn't dressed, still in the pale purple robe, wrapped up tighter this time. She smelled great—much better than the bathhouse soap.

"Schmalch?" she asked. "What're you doing here?"

He jingled the still-damp leather pouch. "That job thing went well. I thought we could go to—"

"Tenta's Fish Fry." She smiled and opened the door. "Come in. I'll switch what I was going to wear—something a little nicer. Oh, I've already applied the red. Still, I have something for that. It'll be perfect. Sit down. I'll be right back." Ooda left the room yet kept talking. "I really liked last time, staying there for the sleebach tournament and all, but I thought this time we could go somewhere different after we eat."

The sleebach tournament had cost Schmalch a quartern's worth of coppers. He didn't mind skipping it.

"Instead, I want to go to the Keepers of the Brine's chapel. The one here in Pukatown, not the big one on Temple Row."

"Wait. What?" He could imagine no reason Ooda would want to visit the Keepers. From everything Schmalch had seen, all they did was send the unclaimed dead back to the sea. A lot of strangers died in Dockhaven, leaving corpses no one knew—or no one loved. So, the Keepers performed the rites and dropped them into the sea. Schmalch got the dithers just thinking he might end up with the Keepers.

"The chapel off Bay Run. They have an oracle. Everybody's been talking about it. I'm surprised you hadn't heard. Yidee said Flerf went and saw him, said he was a real seer, not one of those spooky chivori who never give readings. He told Flerf she'd marry well but lose her husband after only two children. At least she'll be able to feed them. It's proof he speaks truth though. Why else would he tell her about it?"

Schmalch shrugged, trying to decide which spooky chivori she was talking about. Most of the temple-going types were spooky, no matter the species.

"It'll be fun," she said. "Maybe we're fated to be rich."

Schmalch wasn't sure he wanted to know his future. What if it was short? What if things never got better? But he didn't want to disappoint Ooda.

"Um, sure," he said. "How much?"

"With a purse like the one you showed me," she said, twirling into the room in a red dress that fit in all the right places, "you can afford it."

○ ○ ○

They'd eaten well at Tenta's—Schmalch was almost too full. He'd tried to hold back on their spending, but it was tough to skimp in the face of so much good food. He hadn't eaten a meal that big or that tasty in ages. By the time they left, Schmalch was tippled enough to agree to a pedicab when Ooda asked—after all, it *was* a long walk with a belly full of fish, greens, and brew.

The stars were hidden by returning clouds on the ride up Bay Run, so Schmalch and Ooda counted twinkling lights on ships in the anchorage. She snuggled close and told him how good he smelled and how she was hoping the oracle would tell them how gloss life would be. Schmalch couldn't imagine a happier time than this one.

Thunder rumbled in the distance and Ooda tucked her head into his chest. She was so soft. Schmalch hoped the rain wouldn't come back before they were warm together in her bed.

Their driver was huffing when the pedicab stopped in a cloud of smoke that smelled of flowers and corpse rot. The Keepers' chapel was in a rickety-looking old boathouse, the clapboard missing from the dock level, where a scow was moored. It wasn't what Schmalch expected, but some sects were like this—saving their coin for their work instead of building fancy, expensive things that would probably last until Leloloom pulled Dockhaven down into the sea.

In the tiny streetside yard, a pair of Keepers were washing the deck of a tri-wheel used to transport bodies from the lonely places they'd been dumped. One paused to greet them.

"Welcome," he said. "What brings you?"

"We're here to see the oracle," Ooda replied quickly.

"Up the stairs and through the chapel. You'll find him in his sanctum on the bayside."

Ooda made directly for the wooden stairs.

"Grat," Schmalch told the man before scampering to catch up with her.

The pong inside the chapel made Schmalch gag up a reminder of the fish fry. Once, right after Garl had dumped him on Central Row, Schmalch had found a fancy traveler's trunk floating in the bay. He'd imagined it full of swish clothes and jewelry, but when he dragged it to shore and opened it, Schmalch had vomited until he cried. It was full of dead-guy soup. The smell here was the haint of that—with perfume.

Two bodies were laid out on tables at the center of the room, a pair of brown-robed Keepers working on each, black salve smeared under their nostrils and snoots. They all sang quietly in nonsense words as they worked.

Between the tables was a pulley contraption attached to the floor—a platform that moved up and down. Bundles of herbs and flowers hung all over and smoke drifted out of censers at the corners of the room. At the back was a wide altar, lighted candles, seashells, stones, and geegaws littering its top. Shelves along the side walls were packed with bottles of liquid, herbs, and things that looked like they might've come out of a person. Ooda seemed unbothered by any of it.

One body was all strapped up and stitched into sailcloth, almost ready to go back to the sea, a pair of Keepers finishing by painting it with writing. Garl had explained this part to Schmalch once, something about making sure Leloloom would recognize them and not let them drift down to Ruru.

The second body was being washed, its skin pale and loose, like oozing wet cheese. Schmalch guided Ooda toward the side aisle as far from the body as possible, but he couldn't keep from releasing a loud *hurp*, catching the attention of all.

One of the painters, a karju woman, set her brush down and brought a dish to Schmalch and Ooda.

"Here, this will help." She knelt and wiped salve on Schmalch's upper lip. A strong smell like anise candy replaced the death stink. His lip tingled.

"We're here to see the oracle," Ooda said, slapping the woman's hand away when she tried to apply a smear.

The Keeper smiled patiently, reminding Schmalch of Elder Sriree, and gestured toward a door at the back.

"You can go in," she said. "He is alone."

The sanctum was cooler thanks to the open windows, though Schmalch couldn't smell any difference through the salve. A bit of smokiness hung low in the air, tinged blue by lumia lanterns sitting to either side of a rug patterned with what he guessed was seaweed and bubbles. Sitting on a cushion at the far end of the rug, back to a window overlooking the Bay, was a karju man. His long, wavy hair was darker brown than his mustache and beard, the rest of his face obscured by the wriggling light that turned his eyes into dark holes like a skull.

"Sit." The man gestured to cushions at Schmalch and Ooda's feet. "Four coppers, four answers."

Schmalch sat, fished some coins out of his purse, and dropped four into a driftwood offering tray at the rug's edge. Part of him wanted to grab two handfuls from the coins already there and run.

"Only four? What about *your* future Schmalch?" Ooda asked.

"Uh, no," Schmalch said. He didn't really want to know about hundreds more nights drinking at the Barnacle and sleeping in the rain—let alone pay for it.

The oracle picked up a mesh bag and passed it to Ooda.

"Shake the bag while allowing your mind to drift. When you sense it is time, reach in for a handful and cast it on the rug."

As she shook, the oracle sang a creepy tune over and over.

Tingles crawled up Schmalch's back. He lost count of how many times the melody repeated before Ooda sent her handful of geegaws tumbling.

Carrying a long last note, the oracle removed several of the wave-worn shells, stones, bits of glass, chunks of wood, and teeth Ooda had spread in front of him.

"Your children will send you back to sea from Locnor's shore," the oracle said pointing to a bit of seaglass.

"Locnor?" Ooda nearly yelped. "Why would I ever go to Locnor? I hear there's nothing but forests and farms there."

"You follow your mate there, to begin a duck farm." He answered in a plain tone.

"Raising ducks *and* children? That doesn't sound like me. I'm sure I'll have children someday, but mine will be Haveners, just like me—but we'll live on the Big Island or the Nest."

"I do not see the reasons you left Dockhaven," the oracle said, "only that you do leave—and you will be happy."

"Is it a big farm? Will I be rich?"

"It will be a successful endeavor."

"How many children? Who are the fathers?" She seemed to be blurting questions in hopes the oracle would lose count.

"They share a father," he replied. "You and the children send him to the sea a cycle of Dadeyah before your death."

"What's his name? Where does he come from?"

"Four answers have been given." The oracle held out his hand. "The bag."

"Pay him more," Ooda told Schmalch. "Four answers aren't enough."

Schmalch reached for his purse, but the oracle shook his head.

"Four answers, I can give you no more," the oracle told Ooda.

With a huff, she tossed the bag in his lap.

Schmalch felt like he should apologize to the man, but he didn't want to anger Ooda further. Their night had been going so well.

Instead, he started to stand, only to be pulled back down.

"Pay him," Ooda said. "I need to know. Ask him if you're my husband. At least I'll know whether or not to get on a ship with you."

Being Ooda's husband was something Schmalch wasn't sure he wanted. Though he'd like to be her only boyfriend, being a mate and father had never occurred to him. How would he know what to do? Still, he didn't want to sleep under a boat when he could be in a warm bed with Ooda instead. He dropped four more coppers on the tray.

The oracle nodded, scraped all the geegaws off the rug, and dumped them back into the bag, offering it to Schmalch. He sang that creepy song again while Schmalch shook the bag. When the tingles started up his back, Schmalch reached in, grabbed a handful, and tossed. He hoped he liked his four answers better than Ooda had liked hers.

Heart thumping, Schmalch waited while the oracle picked away the extra pieces. When he'd finished, the oracle sat, staring first at the dosh then Schmalch then back again.

Ooda made a little sound like she was about to say something, but the oracle stopped her.

"After standing on many shores," he said, "you will be sent back to the sea from Dockhaven by one who loves you."

Ooda sighed. "That's a relief."

That didn't sound too bad. Someone would love him. Schmalch wasn't sure what to do next—the oracle made him feel like he was sitting there naked—so he looked at the bits spread on the rug. All the geegaws had funny symbols or unrecognizable characters on them. And the ones that were spread across the design were either in a bubble or on one of the connecting fronds of seaweed.

"Do you have any questions for me?" the oracle asked.

Schmalch sucked saliva into his dry mouth. "N-n-no."

The oracle smiled kindly. "That's all right. I see answers unasked for."

He pointed to a bubble with some teeth inside—they looked like they'd once belonged to people, not animals. "You will have a family," the oracle said, "people you live and work with. They will care for you, and you for them."

That sounded pretty swish.

The oracle's hand moved along a seaweed path to an old piece of driftwood. "Before the winter comes, two will lead you into darkness."

That didn't sound so swish—Schmalch would need to be extra careful working with Rothis and Tig.

As the oracle stared at the rug, eyes moving between the geegaws, he started breathing heavily through his nose, like someone being chased by a monster in their dreams. Suddenly, he looked up and leaned so close that Schmalch could finally see his golden eyes, wild and frightening. He studied Schmalch for what seemed like eternity before reaching into the offering tray, removing two coppers, and pressing them into Schmalch's hand.

"I can tell you no more," he said, voice soft and serious. "Go, my friend, let the waves carry you."

Schmalch woke up the next morning in Ooda's bed. The blankets felt amazing. They'd had a nice night after leaving the chapel, though most of the conversation had revolved around Ooda's displeasure with her reading. She was still on it when she woke up.

"We could have been part of the sleebach tournament again," she said first thing. "If Flerf hadn't gone on about how amazing that twitch was, I could have had a lot more fun last night. I'll let her know she best not waste my time with fortune tellers again."

Schmalch felt bad for Flerf, though not enough to say anything.

"What was all that with throwing dosh on a rug? All I know now is to avoid men from Locnor. I do not want to raise ducks for a living."

"Apologies, Ooda." Schmalch shuffled toward the bed's edge, his clothes piled below. If he didn't leave soon, she might decide to be mad at him too.

Ooda rolled out of bed and pulled on the purple robe. "And what was all that plop about you and *great darkness*? These twitching mystics don't actually know squat, so they make up all this cryptic gibberish, and the glints lap it up like caba." She went into the lav, the closed door muffling her voice.

While he dressed, Schmalch found two more stains he hadn't noticed—something beige dribbled down the front of his shirt, and his jacket elbow looked soaked in something dark and reddish, probably caba. Neither stunk, though, so Rothis and Tig shouldn't care.

Ooda cracked the lav door. "Go get us buns while I go through my ablutions."

"Your what?"

"Just buy the buns." She shut the door.

Schmalch dug into his shoe in search of the holdout coins. Though he couldn't remember spending them, they were gone.

He raised his voice. "I, uh, I spent it all last night."

Ooda groaned. After a moment, the door opened, and she stuck out a hand. "Here. Buy the same as yesterday. Knock when you're back." She dropped coins in his palm and shut the door.

When he returned, feeling like the best boyfriend ever, she wouldn't let him in.

"You've got nothing in the hold." She took the buns. "Let me know when that job of yours pays off."

Door shut in his face, Schmalch considered his own breakfast.

He could smell Itnee's all the way from here and his stomach gurgled in response. He couldn't afford even a single bun.

Don't buy what you can steal may have been a Spriggan motto, but there were a lot of extra conditions. The most important was *Don't steal from the Haven's shops*—at least not enough to be noticed. If the Dockhaven Merchant's Guild decided the Spriggans were too big a problem, they could have the orphanage closed—or worse.

Whenever the kids would back-sass her, Elder Tamerlyyn told a story about some city councilor who'd publicly suggested the whole place be burned down—and the rest of the Council had taken her seriously. When she told the story, Tamerlyyn described the councilor as "pale as the Triune, her creases to rival Nugeafu's, her tongue as bitter as Sepmaat's, and a heart that would chill Ruru's." The image had kept Schmalch up at night for at least a quartern. In the end, Tamerlyyn claimed, only its location on the Prick had saved the temple. Toffs didn't really care what happened there as long as their warehouses were safe.

So, Schmalch tried not to steal from the Dockhaven merchants, but this morning he was hungry to the point of distraction. If he did well on this job, maybe Mallow would put him on her regular crew. If he flubbed it, she might sink him or worse, skin him. It was a lot riding on one meal. Too much to risk. So he filched some timnit from a bread cart while the seller was busy helping a customer. This time, Schmalch assured himself, one loaf of bread would be fine. So long as he didn't make it a habit.

The rain returned as little more than a clinging mist, the sun peeking through for heartbeats like a winking eye. People were back out on the streets, more active than they'd been in days. Schmalch thought of his empty pockets and the hours before he had to meet Rothis and Tig at the tram station—then made his way to his favorite blind by the Order of Omatha.

By the time the daylight was fading from the clouds, he'd scaled three marks and had a palmful of coppers to show for it. Schmalch barely resisted the urge to spend a couple at the Barnacle and headed for his meet instead. As he walked through the crowd of day shifters leaving the tram station, he spied Rothis and Tig by the staircase, their arms around one another, her face half-drowned in his bushy beard. Maybe they didn't hate each other after all.

Then Rothis leaned back, said something. Tig's voice rose, and she shoved him away. Rothis backhanded her, and the echo of past smacks stung Schmalch's cheek. Tig staggered back and gave him a rude gesture.

"Vrasaj," Schmalch said too loudly as he walked up. "I'm here."

Tig rubbed the side of her face and said, "Mpf."

"About time, Schmaltz," Rothis said.

"It's not like the building's going to disappear if we get there a little after dark," Tig said.

Rothis glared and she took another step back.

"Yeah, uh, we…" The words froze in Schmalch's throat as their angry eyes turned on him.

Sometimes, when he'd worked with other crews—or even done jobs for Rift and the Duke—he got hurt in the process—but they never did the hurting. He wasn't so sure about these two. He tried not to think about the oracle's promise of *great darkness*.

Schmalch cleared his throat and said quietly, "We should go up before the tram leaves."

Rothis grunted. "Get moving."

Schmalch led them through the process, pleased when he found carriage seats with a view of the city. He liked riding the tram. It was one of the few times he could see just how big Dockhaven was, its chain of islets strung together by bridges, its distant buildings glowing like unspoiled candles. Sometimes he liked to face the Bay mouth and watch the sea, ships of all sizes joining the overflowing population.

Tig and Rothis sat in sullen silence during the ride, unimpressed even when Schmalch pointed out the Gallery of the Nameless on the seaward wall of the Keepers of the Brine's Big Island temple. Hung with the death masks of every Havener the sect had sent to the sea, the wall looked like the faces might spring to life at any moment, moaning and wailing. It was neat and creepy at the same time.

"Pah," Tig said. "Most people deserve to be forgotten."

The Big Island station was much fancier and smelled less like a stale toilet than the one down in the Rabbles. The walls were white here, the attendants dressed in crisp uniforms, the floor free of garbage and mystery spills. The Corps watched *both* the elevators and staircases at this station, it was a terrible spot to do his usual work. He'd tried.

Temple Row was typically quiet at twilight. Most shift workers were already home or at their jobs for the night. Though they passed the occasional temple-goer, no one paid the trio any attention.

Schmalch liked the long, wall-bordered street. It wasn't like any others he traveled. The buildings weren't crowded against one another here. They sat in lush parks of trees, bushes, flowers, fountains, and statues that people like Schmalch could only glimpse through wrought iron gates or barred apertures in the walls. Linger too long at one and guards made sure you went away. He knew all the tops of the buildings that poked above the walls—the Estoan's glass hothouse, the candy-colored tower at the end, and Schmalch's favorite, the Mucha Hall's shiny dome.

"I've heard they have a panther living on the grounds," Schmalch said as they passed the plain, high wall of Seers Abbey. "This guy at the Barnacle told me that if you sneak in, it'll eat you, and no one will ever know."

Rothis snorted. Tig giggled. And Schmalch skipped the rest of his commentary.

The massive Desalinization Plant loomed at the far end of Temple Row. The place was large enough to blot out the horizon, the towers at one end abandoned for as long as Schmalch could remember. Like a giant's corpse the Keepers couldn't haul away, that dead part of the building was creepier than the Gallery of the Nameless any day.

"The lab should be down this way." Schmalch waved for them to follow.

The misty rain had thickened after nightfall, so Schmalch picked up his pace. Rothis and Tig followed him down Ahbo Street, just wide enough for the wains that brought goods to and from the neighborhood. There were no lovely flowers or trees here—all the structures were built right up to the street gutters, wasting no space.

A couple blocks in, they found their destination—a hulk of monotonous grey stone blocks with few windows, *Integrated Zoetics* written on the front in peeling paint. The unshuttered lumia lamps flanking the entrance were dead.

Rothis made them wait at the mouth of an alley that ran alongside the lab until he was sure none of the workers from the nearby buildings would be wandering around. His face looked bland, but the big karju swayed from one foot to the other until the hauler's whistle announced its arrival at the local station.

"Remember, we meet back here. Let's go." Rothis jogged over to the lab door and squatted, jerking his chin at Tig.

She stepped onto his cupped hands, hauling herself up to the window with a soft grunt, and poked a burglar's slim through the upper seal. After fiddling for a moment, something clicked. She tugged and the top swung open.

"Gah! What is that reek?" Tig asked, covering both her snoot and regular nose parts.

Rothis shushed her, his face reddening with the effort of holding her. "Boss said it was a propulsor gestation facility before this. You'll get used to it. Now stop crabbing and do the job."

Schmalch recognized the smell. Back when he'd tried working the wharfs, he'd smelled propulsors all the time. All the big merchant ships had them.

Tig hopped down, nose still covered. Rothis straightened and looked up at the open window.

"Swish work for a farmer's wife," he said, smacking Tig's backside.

Instead of barking in protest, she winked at him.

Schmalch shook his head. He had a lot to learn about relationships.

"Your turn, puka," Rothis said. "When I dump you in, grab the lip and let yourself down. If you miss, try not to fall on anything or yelp."

He grabbed Schmalch around the ribcage so roughly his bones might've cracked. Before he could complain, though, Rothis hefted him up over the window and dropped him in like garbage down a chute. Schmalch scrabbled for the frame's edge, but all his fingers found was a lip too narrow to cling to. He only managed to slow his descent enough to slide halfway down the door before flopping onto the tiled floor. His ass ached, his head rung, and he'd ripped his jacket on the transom's catch.

Schmalch muttered a curse, got to his feet, and waited while his eyes adjusted to the dim light from the transom and curtained window. He'd tumbled into a reception lounge like the kind he'd seen through the windows of the fancy shops on Copper Road—the kind where the real work happened in the backrooms, and the customers rested on cush seating, drinking and nibbling morsels while clerks brought out expensive items one at a time.

No drinking or nibbling here, though—dust was thick on the floor and cobwebs hung limply in corners and from abandoned furniture. No one had enjoyed this lounge in a long time.

The door leading deeper into the building was locked. Rothis hadn't prepared him for that, but a good thief had to be ready for surprises. Schmalch fumbled in his jacket pocket for his picking tools—a bent rod and old hairpin nicked from Elder Tamerlyyn. They weren't fancy, but they'd served him on the few occasions he'd needed them.

Lockpicking had never come easy to him, so work was slow. Schmalch was about to break his hairpin when the cylinder finally rotated. In his excitement, he almost swung the door wide—but caught himself, opening it only enough to peek inside.

The door opened onto a corner where two hallways met—right where he was supposed to be, according to the badly drawn map. Both looked empty, but the dim light from a lumia lamp above the door was quickly gobbled by shadows further down. All the way at the end, the aqua blush of another lamp waited, but in between was murky darkness. Shadows were a lot like people, you couldn't be sure what was hiding inside—and it wasn't easy to know which ones to trust.

According to Rothis, the room he wanted was in that creepy, shadowy area between lights—along with a bunch of other doors behind any one of which could be a guard, a worker, a creature.

He had to go to the commissary first, and that meant going past those dark doors all the way to the end of the hall—then coming back again. The urge to dash through the shadows, down the long corridor, straight to the commissary at the back of the building welled up in him. Despite the flutter in his belly, he knew he had to be patient. Both guards' rounds took them through this corridor, and Schmalch didn't want to run face-first into one as he sped around a corner. So, he waited at the door, peeping through the crack, heart thudding in his ears as he listened for voices or footsteps.

He was about to slip through when he spotted the bobbing white beam of a crank torch turning into the corridor he'd been about to take.

Closing the door—without latching it—he waited until the thwack of boots on tile passed and faded again. Once he was sure the guard was gone, Schmalch slipped into the hallway and hurried into the shadows, hoping he was the only thing they would be hiding.

Moving forward slowly, he dragged his hand along the wall to count rooms. When he ran fingers over the second set of metal double-doors, something behind them made an animal sound—like grunting and gulping at the same time. Schmalch leapt to the far side of the doorway. Rothis said this place wasn't supposed to have any animal guards. Maybe the information was wrong. With a muttered prayer to Tokimer for luck, Schmalch backed away before whatever lived inside that room developed a taste for him.

The third pair of doors—the lab he was supposed to open once he snatched the keys—was fully inside the gloom. His skin prickled as he listened, hearing only soft whirring and bubbling—nothing that sounded like it might eat him. Still, once he had the keys he'd steal a look before slipping inside—quickly, before the grulping thing next door noticed him again.

Schmalch wiped sweaty palms on his pantlegs and drew the kris from its ankle holster. He scratched a small mark on the door and ran a finger over its surface. Even if he couldn't keep count of the rooms on the way back, he'd be able to find the right one.

The thing next door grulped again, causing Schmalch to nearly stab himself in the ankle as he re-sheathed his kris. The monster was still safely behind locked doors, he promised himself, and scurried to the far intersection, watching at the corner to see if the guard's torch would return before crossing into the light.

The commissary doors were already open, the big room inside mostly dark. In the lone island of lamplight sat the other guard—a lanky karju man, his boots propped on the tabletop, nose in a book. Schmalch dropped to hands and knees and crawled under the first table in the string between them, pausing beneath each to be sure he wasn't noticed. When he reached the pool of light surrounding his target, he hesitated a few heartbeats longer.

Schmalch slipped into the light, staying in the man's blind spot—that same overlooked area shared by all species with such weirdly placed eyes. He crept close, pleased by how well he was executing the plan, and dove into the shadows under the table. Clipped to a belt loop on the guard's black coveralls, a fat keyring dangled within reach like so many snatched purses.

All Schmalch had to do now was press the catch and lift the keys without tugging or jingling. He was used to city noise covering his work, and it was silent here—but he was a good thief. He could be as quiet as a street cat. Schmalch held his breath and reached.

The man shifted, farted, and closed his book. "Time to feed the dibucs," he muttered, pushing his chair back and walking toward the open door. Schmalch jerked his hand back and held his nose.

While he waited for the guard to return, Schmalch wondered if Rothis and Tig were getting impatient for him to finish his part. If they were, he couldn't do much about it besides apologize. He shrugged his still-sore shoulder and hoped Rothis wouldn't dangle him again.

Soon enough, boots slapped back toward the table, black pantlegs appeared, and a woman's voice grumbled, "Where'd he get off to?" She sniffed. "Gah! Shitting again."

The first guard, Schmalch guessed, back from her rounds.

He barely dodged a kick when she dragged out a chair and sat down, stretching her too-long legs beneath the table.

"What drivel is he reading this time?" she asked herself. "*Phantoms of the White Moon.* Another pile of birdlime." She snickered and dropped the book on the table with a thump that made Schmalch's heart leap into his throat.

She started leafing through the book, snorting and chuckling at what she found.

He was getting ready to reach for her keys when the other guard returned.

"Hey," the man said, "don't lose my place."

"Like I'd read that twaddle," she replied. "Don't bother to sit down, it's time for you to check on the squints upstairs."

"Alright. Mark my page." He paused. "Seriously, don't lose it."

"Fine. Just go."

Schmalch heard the fading whir of a torch being cranked as the man left.

The woman whistled raspily and adjusted, forcing Schmalch to duck beneath her chair. After a moment, he leaned out for a better view of the keys clipped to her beltloop. Simple enough. Schmalch gently cupped them in one hand and fingered the hook's catch with the other. With a soft *tink*—covered by the guard's whistling—they dropped into his palm. He grinned. Now he just needed to escape before either guard wandered through the commissary again.

Schmalch scrambled out from under the chair, scurrying silently under the line of tables. He didn't pause at the door, just hoped the patrolling guard was far away. Gut anticipating a shout, he darted out of the commissary, heading deep into hallway. The shadows were his friends now, not nearly as scary as being caught and thrown in the Bag. Halfway to the target lab, he straightened and side-shuffled along the wall until he reached the marked door.

He tried key after key, handling them carefully—he didn't want to attract the guard or disturb the grulping thing next door—but none of them seemed to work. He'd tried at least half when boot steps echoed through the sleeping building. The was guard on the last leg of his rounds. The corridor was bare—no furniture, no potted plants, no way of hiding from a crank torch on this side of the door. Schmalch had to hurry. When another key failed, he nearly cried, unable to ignore the steps closing in on him. He wanted to rush, but that meant jangling keys, and that would only bring the guard faster.

He could do this. He was a good thief.

His palms slick with nerve-sweat, the next key Schmalch tried clicked into place. He slipped into the lab quickly, easing the door closed as the guard's torchlight panned over the hall.

Schmalch sagged against the door. He'd nearly blown the whole thing and ended up in the Bag, not a single copper richer. But he didn't. He was a good thief.

The familiar smell of propulsor hung in the air, thick enough to taste. The lab was smaller than he'd expected, most of it filled by two glowing greenish glass tubes, three pukas tall and as wide as a brew vat. Floating inside each was a ropy young propulsor, puckered mouth at either end. They reminded him of the big hose Elder Eliigia used in the garden—but alive and many times thicker. He tried not to look right at them as he scanned the room for his target.

No safe in sight, but some dark shapes at the far end of the room showed promise. Checking them out meant he'd have to walk past the propulsor tanks. Schmalch didn't really want to do that. What if the glass broke? A bilge drudge had once told him about the bloody mess left after a crewmate shot through one. Propulsors weren't mean, the drudge had assured Schmalch, they just wanted to do the one thing they were designed to do—suck up seawater in front and shoot it out their back end. They were just *indiscriminate*, the drudge said. Schmalch wasn't entirely sure what that meant, but he understood not to stand too close to a propulsor's mouths.

These two were small, not like the big ones in ships that could turn a puka into chunks and mist. He'd dash through the room and be past them in a wink. He'd be fine. He had to do it—if he left this place without the sample, Rothis would give him far worse than the back of his hand. And who knew what he'd owe Sigrin for flubbing up twice in a row.

Schmalch gulped air and scuttled past the tanks, trying not to look but unable to avoid doing so. He nearly yelped when one of the wormy propulsors shifted in its tank, both toothless mouths pulsing at him like a baby searching for a teat. He burst from between the tanks and ran past a pair of worktables into the open area at the room's rear. A couple of desks, one cluttered, one tidy, faced the wall. A squat safe sat off to one side. On the wall above it twinkled a panel filled with shiny buttons, switches, and winking lights. A big lever in the middle begged to be pulled.

Another one of Elder Sriree's lessons echoed Schmalch's head: "Get what you need and get out. If it isn't going to put food in your belly, don't worry about it."

Still, he wondered what that lever did. Would it make the red light at the top turn a different color? Go out? Would a new one come on?

He dragged one of the desk chairs over and climbed up, examining the lever. The lights blinked on and off at different rates. Orange was fast, and green almost kept up, but yellow seemed sleepy. The red one never turned off. Did they all mean something or were they just there to be pretty?

His eyes drifted back to the shiny lever. One little tug wouldn't hurt. *Then* he'd find the sample.

Schmalch licked his lips and touched the lever. It was cold and smooth like Garl's brew vats. As Schmalch wrapped his fingers around the handle, something thudded behind him. He leapt off the chair and dove under a desk, ready to defend against being captured or eaten. No one stood there, but that same propulsor was rubbing its mouths against the glass again, still searching for something to clamp onto.

What if the lever opened that thing's tube?

Elder Sriree had been right—grab the sample and leave. Schmalch could find different levers to pull some other time— though none nearly as swish.

He jumped off the chair and squatted by the safe. It had two keyholes, just like Rothis had said, but they were weird, three-pronged. He'd never seen anything like them before. With his kris, Schmalch notched the key for the lab door—in case he needed it again in a hurry—and flipped through the rest of the ring. Most featured the standard one- or two-prong arrangement, but a pair of brass keys had three.

He inserted and turned one key then the other, each ratcheting into place. But the wheel wouldn't budge. Schmalch's stomach and throat tightened. These were the only two keys with three prongs—they had to work. His breathing sped up. These had to be the right ones. What had he done wrong? Rothis' voice popped into his head, "…turn them at the same time, can you remember that?"

Schmalch spun the keys back to their start and cranked them together. Something inside went *clonk* and the wheel turned. He really was a good thief. Mallow would have to make him part of her crew after he did such a gloss job. Wouldn't that scorch Sigrin?

Everything inside the safe was papers or books, only the sample case stood out. Blacker than a new moon night, it was about the size of the colorful all-day sweets the elders used to pass out for Reapers and Sowers festivals. He missed those treats.

Behind him, the propulsor thumped again on the tank wall. A little tickle of fear ran up Schmalch's spine. The scientists grew them without eyes. That seemed mean.

Schmalch pocketed the black ball and scurried past the propulsor tanks, pausing to peek out the door instead of leaping right back into the hallway. No footsteps, no voices, not even the grulping monster in the next room made a sound. He eased the lab door open and slipped into the empty corridor.

No guards appeared, and Schmalch made it back to the front door undetected. He shuffled through the keyring again, picking the right one on his first guess this time—the same one that had opened the lab door. Rothis and Tig were probably done cutting the alarm and waiting outside, wondering where he was. He hoped they weren't mad.

Schmalch stuck his head out the front door. The rain started again—or the mist had gotten so heavy it had begun to fall—but nobody was waiting for him in the alley's mouth, where Rothis said they'd meet.

Schmalch closed the door and wiped the rain off his nose. Rothis said they were going to turn off the alarm, nothing else.

Maybe they had something else important to do but didn't mention it—some secret mission from Mallow. Maybe they got caught. No, he would have heard the noise if those two had been captured. More likely, they got mad and left when he'd been so slow. Maybe he should go looking for them. No, better to wait here as he'd been told.

Schmalch squatted by the front door and ignored his grumbling stomach. At least he was warm and dry. He wondered if Mallow would still pay him the full three Callas after Rothis fronted all those coppers. Either way was fine with him, though he'd prefer to have both. Once he'd been paid, he could afford to take Ooda to the Fish Fry again and stay for the sleebach tournament this time. He could buy Plu a new shocker instead of chancing Dinnlit selling him a dud with bad caps. He might even buy a night or two at a swish place like the Belvedor—though the idea of sleeping in a room all by himself seemed kind of spooky.

A wandering whistle echoed down the hall, less raspy than the woman's. The lanky guard was getting close.

Schmalch poked his head out the front door again. Rothis and Tig were nowhere to be seen. Hard as he listened, all he heard were the night sounds of the city, the whistle and boot-slap of the approaching guard, and his own frantic breathing. Had they been captured? Were they dead? He resisted the urge to bolt out into the street and race back down to the Rabbles.

Instead, he opened the interior door and chanced a peek down the hallways. The guard was strolling along, shining his torch on every door as he passed. Schmalch was pretty sure he'd closed the lab when he left.

Did the guard look into the lounge when he passed? Or did he walk right on by? Schmalch could hide under some of the dusty furniture, but it was still a risk. If he got grabbed here, he'd be in the Bag by sunrise, the black ball confiscated by the Corps. Better to deliver the sample to Mallow tomorrow than lose it tonight.

Schmalch slipped outside and ran for the shadows they'd stood in earlier, rain streaming cold trails down his skull, soaking his clothes yet again. Behind him, the front door swung open, and the whistling guard stepped out. Schmalch didn't bother waiting, he scuttled down the alley, away from capture.

As he neared an intersection, he heard the echoing rumble of a deep voice, dulled by the pattering rain. Schmalch hesitated and listened before rounding the corner.

"…be here after the horn blew," said the voice.

Rothis. Schmalch almost cheered.

"Malpockey said he'd be here," he continued. "Maybe he got twitchy and someone noticed."

"Maybe your distraction didn't work." Tig's voice sounded hollow bouncing between buildings.

"You think he's been nicked by now?" Rothis asked.

"Obviously. You saw how clumsy he was."

"It should've been simple," Rothis said. "Distraction up front, meet around back."

Schmalch shook his head. He must have forgotten part of the plan and left through the wrong door. They'd expected him to come out the back.

"Well, he's not here. Great plan," Tig said, followed by the smack of skin on skin.

Schmalch stepped out of the alley. Rothis and Tig were standing under a faded awning above a big metal door, drizzle around them glowing in the ghostly streetlight. They looked miserable.

"I'm here!" Schmalch said a little too loudly, his voice bouncing down the surrounding network of alleyways.

Both turned on him. Tig drew a short knife.

"Son of a dibuc," Rothis said, fists relaxing. The rain beads in his beard made him look sparkly. "What're you doing back here?"

"I'm finished," Schmalch said. "I guess I went out the wrong door when I was done. Apologies."

Rothis and Tig looked at each other and laughed.

"You have the sample?" Tig asked.

Schmalch patted his pocket. "Right here."

"Imt's eyes," Rothis muttered. "What about the keys?"

"Them too."

"Give 'em to me."

Schmalch tossed the keys to Rothis, who started trying one after another in the back door's lock.

"I scratched a notch in the one that opened the lab," Schmalch said. Even if he wasn't sure why they wanted inside, at least he could be helpful. "It worked on the front door too. You should try that one."

Rothis gave him a dark look, but the key worked. He eased the back door open, stuck his head in, and looked around.

"C'mon Tiggy," he said. "The stairs are close and no one's in sight. We're gonna go snatch us a zoeticist."

Tig looked like she'd eaten bad fruit. "Can you even remember where his quarters are?"

"Of course I can. Now get in here."

"There's a guard on rounds," Schmalch said, wondering how he'd missed even more of the plan. He thought they were supposed to leave now.

"You're on lookout, puka." Rothis grabbed Schmalch's jacket and pulled him inside. "Stick right here by the door until we get back. "

Schmalch had never been the best lookout. He tended to run when trouble appeared instead of alerting others. Nevertheless, he nodded.

Rothis and Tig disappeared into the stairwell's open mouth.

Schmalch looked around. Everything was quiet. Dimly, he could hear the rain pattering outside. No whistling or bootsteps, though. He squatted by the door, itchy in his wet clothes.

What exactly were they doing? Rothis said, "snatch us a

zoeticist." Did that mean they were stealing a person too? Schmalch shook his head. That didn't seem right. Someone would have mentioned that.

Or—maybe he hadn't missed anything at all, and this was a plan known only to Mallow's crew. If she liked Schmalch's work and picked him up, maybe he'd be in on secrets like that too. He'd done his job. Aside from using the wrong door, he'd done everything he'd been told. She'd put him on the crew for sure.

He pulled the black ball out of his pocket. It didn't look like impressive boodle, but its insides were obviously worth lots more than the three Callas Schmalch was earning. Pale lines ran across its surface, so thin they were barely there. Seams maybe? Or decorations? Sometimes the elders would decorate the festival candies, but nothing as fancy as this. He wondered if the black ball tasted like those candies. Probably not—but still, it might. Tig had said the sample was inside a bottle that couldn't be opened without a special bath. She said it wouldn't hurt him.

Schmalch popped the ball into his mouth, rolling it over his tongue. Not sweet or sour, it tasted as bland as the marbles he used to be punished for swallowing. The dibucs couldn't break them down, the elders said, so anytime Schmalch ate a marble, they put him on lav duty, cleaning bowls and changing tanks.

Sudden, loud footsteps thunked nearby—one set, coming from a side hall just past the stairwell. Schmalch jumped to his feet. In a heartbeat, the beam of a crank torch flashed across the wall ahead. Should he run up the stairs? Duck back outside? Shout? Rothis had only told him to stay, not what to do if anyone showed up.

The lady guard wheeled around the corner, her torch catching Schmalch cowering by the door. Her eyes widened. "Wha—?" She drew a pistol from a shoulder holster.

Schmalch hadn't noticed they were armed.

"You!" the guard shouted. "Hands where I can see them."

He was a terrible thief. He was going to die.

"Hands!" she hollered and stepped closer.

Schmalch raised his hands and backed into the unlocked door, which swung open, sending him tumbling into the street with a splash. The sample lurched in his mouth and he swallowed automatically. The black ball lodged in his throat. Unable to breathe, Schmalch gulped and gulped again, bruising his insides as the sample worked its way to his stomach.

The guard stepped into the open doorway. "Stop right there or I shoot!"

Schmalch froze, still gulping.

Rothis appeared behind her, palmed the side of her head, and smashed it into the door jamb. Half the guard's face collapsed like rotten fruit, blood spraying into the rain. She released a wet *yerk* and went limp.

As Rothis rolled her body into the alley with his foot, Schmalch scuttled back to avoid the gore and got to his feet. Tig joined them, one hand clamped on the upper arm of a wide-eyed karju man in pajamas and robe. Schmalch guessed it was the zoeticist Rothis had mentioned.

"Sweet Mother Jajal, what have you done?" The captive man's words came out in a bumble. "I'm not doing this, no one was supposed to get hurt. Just go and tell Marthoth I've changed my mind. I won't tell anyone I saw you." He pulled against Tig's grip, trying to go back toward the stairs.

Rothis grabbed the zoeticist's robe, tossed him in a puddle, and kicked him in the gut.

"If you'd been where you were supposed to be, I wouldn't have had to hurt anybody." He pointed to the dead guard. "So, that's on you."

"I- I- I-" the man stammered, clutching his gut.

Rothis hoisted the zoeticist to his feet by one arm and shoved him forward. "No more hysterics, Behaani. We're going"

Tig squatted, grabbed the guard's dropped pistol, and waved it at Schmalch. "You too. Let's go, thief."

Schmalch jogged to keep up as Rothis marched blindly through the neighborhood, one hand knotted in Behaani's collar. He was in charge, so everyone followed him—but Schmalch could tell Rothis knew almost nothing about Dockhaven's layout. He turned down blind alleys, went in circles, and cursed a lot.

When they emerged from the warren of industrial buildings at the backside of Temple Row, Rothis stopped and punched the Estoan Lodge's outwall.

"Punky-keeled son of a whore!" he screamed at the sky.

Slipping from his grasp, Behaani wheeled, his rain-soaked robe clinging to him so tightly that Schmalch could see the outline of something big in his pocket.

"You don't even know where you're taking me!" Behaani shrieked. "Do you know what Integrated Zoetics does to defectors? Mister Marthoth can buy the vaccine for his propulsors when it comes to market like everyone else. Take me back!"

Rothis grabbed fistfuls of the robe, slamming the man into the outwall. "You're staying right here. Now, keep it corked. I'm trying to think."

"They'll lock me away on some research vessel in the Middle Sea—if they decide I have any value left." Behaani found his robe pocket and tugged at whatever was inside, the wet cloth clinging like a net. With a grunt and rip of fabric, he pulled out a widemouthed scattershot pistol, all black wood and shiny silver.

Before the zoeticist could bring the pistol to bear, Tig fired the dead guard's weapon. Behaani's head snapped back, a chunk missing where his eye had been. He lingered a moment, mouth working, then dropped. Brains and splinters of bone speckled the bloody splash left behind, rain drizzling it all slowly down the outwall.

Everything was silent for three beats—then Rothis erupted. With a roar, he dropped the corpse, slapped the pistol from Tig's hand, and smashed her against the gory wall, throat squeezed in his enormous hand.

"What in Wetac's madness were you thinking?" he hollered in her face, rainwater and spit flying from his moustache and mouth. Little bits of Behaani were stuck in his hair and beard.

Tig clawed at his arm and croaked, "He was going to shoot you."

Rothis released his grip, letting her slide down the wall, her hair and jacket collecting the mess left by the dead scientist. She slumped in the streaming gutter and cried—or pretended to. Schmalch couldn't tell.

Rothis paced in a circle like a caged predator. "It was a simple job. Dump in our bait animal to set off the alarm so the guards head to the front. Meet the zoeticist and his sample at the back door, escort him to the Upper Rabble, and get paid. Simple."

He turned on Schmalch, fists balled. "Until this douse did what he was told, the target had a change of heart, and my partner shoots him through the twitching head!"

"What's all this then?" A Corpsman emerged from a nearby alley, hand on the gun at his hip.

Tig rolled, grabbed Behaani's scattershot pistol, and fired. Her shot went wide—only a few pellets cratered the Corpsman's shoulder—but it was enough to send him staggering back with a shout.

Red-faced, Rothis bellowed, "Stop shooting people!" and kicked the swish gun out of Tig's hand. It skittered across the cobbles, stopping at Schmalch's feet.

Blood darkening his rain-soaked uniform, the Corpsman righted himself and grabbed his pistol—but Rothis was faster. He drew his dagger and threw it like a carnival performer. The shiny blade sunk into the Corpsman's chest with a wet *thwack*. He dropped his pistol and pawed at Rothis' knife, blood bubbling from his mouth. He stared at them—surprised, afraid—fell to his knees, and tipped limply to one side.

"Imt's eyes," Rothis swore. "We need to move before another one comes along." He put one foot on the Corpsman's chest and pulled the blade out with a sucking *slarp*.

Schmalch snatched Behaani's scattershot pistol and followed, grateful for the deep pockets of his new jacket. He'd net a bunch of Callas for such a swish gun.

"Puka," Rothis said, "take us back to the Rabbles."

"Um…" Schmalch looked around.

They were behind Temple Row. Going past the Corps at the tram station was a bad idea. Even with the rain, there was a good chance someone would notice the blood on Tig and Rothis, and Schmalch had never been good at bluffing his way past suspicious glances. So, he led them to the nearest water taxi slip, a short way down the Pipe.

Rothis paid the fare and waggled a Calla at the pilot. "Keep your eyes forward and your trap shut, and this'll be yours when we get to the other side of the Bay. You catch?"

The pilot nodded, pink rain hat flopping and dribbling, and started pedaling like two of his passengers weren't covered in gore. A dock so close to the Bag probably attracted plenty of less-savory types than them.

For a while, they rode quietly. Schmalch closed his eyes and focused on the whir of the boat's gearbox, trying to calm the fear tangling his belly.

They were passing the Bag when Rothis asked, "You have the sample, right?"

"He probably lost it in that mess you made," Tig said.

Rothis didn't bother to look when he backhanded her, just kept staring at Schmalch.

"Uh huh," Schmalch said. It wasn't quite a lie. "I have it,"

"Give it to me."

"Um."

Rothis' eyes narrowed. His beard quivered. "Hand it over."

"I can't."

"But you do still have it?"

"Yeah."

Rothis growled.

"Sweet Mother Jajal," Tig said. "The little douse swallowed it."

Schmalch looked at his feet and nodded.

Rothis drew his dagger, the Corpsman's blood still around the hilt.

Schmalch released a pained whine. He was a good thief. He'd stuck to the plan and done everything they asked—even since the job went belly-up, and still, they were still gonna slice him open. Now, he was trapped between Rothis and a cold swim to the Bag. They didn't bother to arrest you for trespassing on prison grounds, just shoved you into a cell with a bunch of cutthroats. No matter what he did, he was doomed to end up there.

He had one last option—the best, even if it was still terrible. Schmalch could manage a swim to a nearby ship and hope they'd let him aboard. He hopped out of his seat and jumped, *almost* making it over the side before Rothis caught his sore arm and yanked him down to the deck.

"A puka's stomach is right about here, isn't it Tig?" Rothis said, tracing the tip of the knife across Schmalch's middle.

Something sour rose in Schmalch's throat. He felt nauseous. Maybe the black ball hadn't been as safe as he'd been told.

Tig grabbed Rothis' wrist. "We already have three bodies in our wake and one of them was the law around here. Do you really want to perform surgery in this boat?"

He shook her off. "This won't be surgery, more like gutting a boar."

"Fine, be an imbecile. What about him?" She gestured at the pilot. "Do you think he's going to take your Calla and stay quiet about his boat full of puka guts? Or are you going to kill him too?"

The pilot stopped pedaling.

"We're both covered in blood as it is," Tig continued. "We'll be lucky to make it down the pier without the Corps noticing us. And if they do, you know what I'm going to say? 'Help me officer, he just went berserk and killed all those people.'"

Rothis' grip relaxed. He looked at Tig. "You'd really do that, wouldn't you?"

She nodded.

He sneered at Schmalch. "I'm gonna let you up. Try to get away again, and I'll put this knife through your neck before you make it two steps."

"You got it, Rothis," Schmalch said. "I'll stick with you."

"I need to think." Rothis slumped into his seat. "We can't go back to Malpockey like this. We'll be lucky if she doesn't kill us, let alone pay us."

Tig put her arm around him, head on his shoulder. "I know, Growler."

"Let's go back to the Belvedor."

"Malpockey knows we're staying there," Tig said. "When we don't come back on time, she'll send her goon there first to find us."

Rothis shook her off. "Imt's eyes, woman. I don't know then. I told you I need to think."

"I, uh, I know a place we might be able to stay," Schmalch said quietly. Ooda wouldn't like it, but he could spend all three Callas on her to make up for using her cuddy. "Only if you promise not to gut me. It'll come out eventually, you know—the sample, I mean. Just like the marbles used to."

"Fine," Rothis said. "When this thing lands, take us there and I won't gut you."

"Promise?"

"Sax's tit. Yes, I promise."

"Drop us off at the Runoff." Schmalch told the pilot, who nodded and resumed pedaling.

The rain tapered off as they traveled across the harbor, the clouds clearing by the time they reached the floater neighborhood. Looking at Tig and Rothis, Schmalch wished for a downpour long enough to wash away their gory splotches. Ooda would never let them in looking the way they did.

Schmalch told the taxi driver to drop them off at a fishers dock where they could clean up with a seawater handpump. The locals used them to spray away fish guts and other dreck, but they'd work just as well on karju bits.

After hosing them off, he led them into the maze of lashed-together razees, pontoons, houseboats, and hovel-rafts that separated them from the shore.

"What in the depths is this place?" Tig asked when Schmalch stopped on the gangway between two darkened shacks to decide which way to turn next.

"The Runoff," Schmalch said, scampering in the direction most likely to lead to shore.

Tig followed. "That doesn't explain anything. In fact, I have more questions now."

"Keep it down," Rothis growled from behind them. "We don't need to wake up the locals."

Schmalch lowered his voice and gestured to the intertwined fleet of wrecks around them. "People move in, people move out. Layout's always changing." Which made it a good place to hide.

"Why?"

"Too expensive inland, I guess." He paused, trying to figure the best route. "Or they like it? I don't know."

"And the name?"

Schmalch pointed. "The Slaughteryards are up the coast."

"I know that, but—" Her face contorted with disgust. "Sax! They just put it in the water? Is that what I've been smelling?" She gagged. "This place. This twitching place."

"You two, cork it until we get where were going," Rothis hissed.

When they reached the far side of Pukatown, Ooda laughed in

Schmalch's face.

"Oh my, that's the best joke I've heard in days," she said. "You really have overestimated your credit, Schmalch. No, you and your cagey-looking friends cannot squat in my place. I already have company."

The sailor from a few days ago moved into view behind her.

"I'm making three Callas off this job," Schmalch said. "I'll give them to you if you just let us stay here a little while. We'll be quiet. You'll hardly notice us."

"First off, you know my bung doesn't allow karju," Ooda said. "And I'm not going to have them stomping around, breaking up the place and gamming off the neighbors."

"We can sit," Tig said. "Just for a little while. You'll hardly notice us."

Ooda snorted. "Second, you're soaking wet and filthy. And were you rolling in garbage water? I don't want that in my home. Third—"

"Lash that down, trull," Rothis said. "We're coming in." He shoved Ooda out of the way with a palm to the face and bulled into her apartment.

She shrieked. The sailor inside shouted.

The door across the hall opened and a man with a streetball stick stared at Schmalch.

"You thugs leave Ooda alone. Bradit!" he called behind him. "Ring the bell and call the Corps."

Schmalch tugged Rothis' coat. "We need to go. It won't take them long."

They all ran, Tig shouting nasty names Schmalch had never heard before at Ooda and her neighbors.

"Don't ever come back here again, Schmalch," Ooda yelled down the stairs after him. "Or we'll leave you in the gutter for the Keepers."

By the time they made it to the street, most of the building's tenants were ringing bells out their windows. It seemed like all of Pukatown was awake now. The Corps would be there in heartbeats. Schmalch ran, barely caring if Tig and Rothis were behind him.

A few streets away, Schmalch spied a near-empty bar he'd never been to. But off the street was better than on until the neighborhood settled down. He ducked inside and waved the two karju after him.

"If you're not drinking you can move along now," said the sleepy-eyed dodder manning the place. "This isn't a flop."

Rothis locked eyes with the old lady, and for a moment Schmalch thought he might kill her too. When she gave him a toothless smile, though, Rothis shook his head.

"Three brews," he told her.

They settled in a booth toward the back and slouched over their mugs, each keeping their own thoughts. As soon as the din died down outside, Schmalch wanted to run. The Corps probably wouldn't be motivated into a door-to-door search by an argument at a Pukatown apartment, but they might put out more Corpsmen. If one of them came in here for a drink…

Rothis knocked his empty mug against the scarred tabletop signaling the barkeep to bring another.

"We're heading into the depths." Rothis shifted, locking eyes with Schmalch. "I don't see a way back up that doesn't come down to cutting you open."

Schmalch's stomach lurched. It felt like the ball was trying to come back up but wouldn't fit. He wished it would—maybe the surprise hork would give him a chance to scramble out of reach.

"Imt's eyes, you are the stupidest bull in the pen," Tig said. "Should we get a couple of these ancient tipplers to hold him down while you slice him open?"

Rothis' hand shot across the table and clamped onto her face, fingers pressed deep. "*I'm trying to think*," he growled, spittle dripping from his lower lip. "So, why don't you cork it for once in your miserable life, farmer's wife?"

Under the table, Tig jammed her boot into Rothis' groin. He let go with an *oof*. Big purple ovals from his fingers lingered on her cheeks.

"I'm done with you," Tig said. "I'll reeve my way back to Imtnor if I have to."

"Good luck with that, Tigania. You're too mouthy and too needy to be a good trull."

Tig slapped him.

Rothis grabbed her by the hair and pulled her close. "I coulda moved on, joggled some other miserable dandle, but I wound up with you. I don't care how good you reeve, you put me in charge, so I'm in charge. You're not running. We're going back to Malpockey. That fid Behaani got himself killed. We explain that, take our licks, find something else."

"She'll kill us."

Rothis shook his head. "We still have the sample."

They both looked at Schmalch.

Panic crawled up his back. He was trapped between Rothis, the table, and the wall. Grabbing for his kris, Schmalch tried to slide under the table. Before he could draw his weapon or escape, Tig swung her mug.

Jostled into woozy consciousness, Schmalch found himself slung over Rothis' shoulder with a view of the hairy thug's back. His wrists and ankles were tied with rough cord. The cloth jammed in his mouth tasted of dishwater and stale brew, and he could feel the empty sheath of his kris pressed against his ankle.

He raised his aching head as much as the pain would allow. They were on Central Row, already surrounded by the sheet metal hulks of Marthoth Air & Sea's warehouses. He was sunk—tied up, gagged, his kris gone. Soon he—like its last owner—would be dead.

A shadow crossed their wake, scrambling from one alley mouth to another. Probably just a cat, but Schmalch wondered if it was one of the Jykiini lying in wait to run off with his spirit.

When they arrived, Warehouse 4 reverberated with the slow rhythm of the night shift. Peppered among the workers, cruel faces watched the pair and their catch. One met Schmalch's eyes and sliced a red thumb across her throat. The Band of the Bloody Thumb, the nastiest gang in the Upper Rabble, were hanging around. That was weird. Maybe they'd kill Sigrin for being in their territory—a nice parting thought for Schmalch to take to Dormah when he died.

Rothis jogged up the stairs to Mallow's office, shoulder digging into Schmalch's gut with each step. He might have spewed down the karju's back if the black ball hadn't felt like it was lodged at the entry to his stomach. When Rothis dropped Schmalch into a chair, the ball seemed to sink back into his bilge. Schmalch tried to stand up and run, but Rothis clamped his shoulder against the chair with an iron grip.

Mallow sat at her desk, tired eyed, scary guard to one side, her douse of a brother on the other. All three looked confused.

Sigrin snorted. "Not dead or in the Bag yet Schmalchy? The badger must—"

His sister shut him up with a raise of her hand. "What in the name of Ruru's cold, clammy quim is this?" she asked.

"The puka snagged the sample," Rothis said.

Mallow's eyes narrowed. "Where's the zoeticist? What's his name, Siggy?"

"Behaani," Sigrin said.

"Him. Where is he?"

Rothis cleared his throat, hand tightening on Schmalch's shoulder. "He's dead."

Mallow leaned forward on the desk. "What did you say?" Her voice was low and scary.

"A Corpsman shot him," Rothis said, quickly adding, "Behaani shot first."

"He had a gun? Why did the twitch have a gun? Wait—did you say he shot a *Corpsman*?"

Rothis nodded.

"Did he kill him?"

Rothis hesitated, hand squeezing the blood out of Schmalch's shoulder.

"Yeah," he said.

The lie hung there quietly.

"Let *me* explain," Tig said.

Rothis growled at her.

"It was arsy-varsy from the start," Tig continued. "Behaani didn't show up like you said he would. We were just standing around back waiting in the rain. Nobody opened the door. Nobody knocked. Nothing."

Mallow's eyes flicked between them. "You went to the *back* door?"

"We dropped the puka in up front and ran around back," Tig said. "Behaani wasn't there. So, we decided to go in and snatch him, bring him back like you said."

Mallow's eyes shifted to Schmalch. "Let's hear what the puka has to say. Take that rag out of his mouth."

Rothis gave Schmalch another warning squeeze and pulled the gag out, never letting go of the shoulder.

"And you were where?" Mallow asked.

"I scaled the keys and ball—sample, I mean—but then I must've gone to the wrong door," Schmalch said. "I thought we were supposed to meet out front, but they were around back, so I wasn't there on time, but I found them and gave them the keys."

Rothis cleared his throat again. "Yeah."

"So, I have a gudgeon who actually did his job and a pair of dunders who got their charge killed. Is that accurate?"

"He didn't show," Tig protested. "If Behaani had been where he was supposed to be, then everything would have gone perfectly. We weren't prepared for the break-in because nobody told us it was possible we'd need those tools."

"If you'd gotten the gen right," Rothis added, "we would have brought what we needed for a snatch."

Mallow's brows went up. "Jeho, deal with the door," she said.

The guard nodded and crossed the room. As he passed, Jeho pulled something from his belt and jammed it into Rothis' midsection. Schmalch felt a nasty tingle run through the restraining hand before it suddenly let go of his shoulder. When Schmalch looked behind him, Rothis was on his knees, and the room smelled like lightning. Schmalch almost laughed. A shocker—just like Plu wanted.

"Now that you understand what I think of excuses," Mallow turned to Tig, "where's the sample?"

"The puka swallowed it," Tig blurted.

Getting back to his feet, Rothis glared at her.

Mallow leaned back in her chair, massaging her eyes. "I could have hired Toh, but my brother said he knew 'just the people' and dragged you in here. And you convinced me you were professionals."

"We are." Rothis grumbled.

"And neither of you dunders thought to make him throw it up?"

"It almost got stuck going down," Schmalch said quietly.

"Of course it did. This is the last time I trust your judgement, Siggy." Mallow threw a marking stick at her brother's head. "Don't just stand there like a lump. Go fetch Helik."

With a menacing smirk for Schmalch, Sigrin left.

Schmalch recognized the name—a chop doc who anchored in the Lower Rabble. Mallow was going to cut him open, take the sample, and leave him bleeding with his guts slopped on the floor. Forgetting his bound ankles, Schmalch tried to bolt, instead falling hard to the floor. His mind grasped frantically for reasons she should keep him alive—he didn't eat much, he'd done what she told him, he was a good thief—but the only sound his throat would make was a frightened whine.

"Jeho," Mallow said, "puka."

Lightning burst bright in the back of Schmalch's skull and everything went black.

○○○

Schmalch woke to the smell of a piss-filled cat box. He was lashed to a steel table, bar cloth stuffed back in his mouth, his damp shirt pulled up to expose his belly. Over him stood a karju man he'd never seen before, waving a stinky little box under Schmalch's nose. Darker and better dressed than the others, he wore wire-rimmed spectacles with dozens of little lenses like the physician who used to visit the Spriggans.

"Calm yourself. Struggling will just make it worse," the stranger said in a voice like a warm blanket.

"Since you're an expert on innards, Helik," Mallow said, "I figured if you couldn't make him spew the sample case, you could cut him open and dig it out. Easy enough, right?"

Schmalch's heart was beating so hard he could feel it in his eyeballs. He needed to do something, or he'd be skewered before the sun rose. As best he could, Schmalch scanned the room. They were still in Mallow's office. She, Rothis, Tig, Sigrin, and the guard were all standing around watching like gawkers at an accident. He saw no options for escape.

Another wave of nausea hit and the ball pushed painfully into a spot just under Schmalch's heart before falling back into his bilge. The chop doc studied Schmalch, one brow raised, before removing the multi-specs.

"No," Helik said. "Given the size of the foreign body, there's a high risk he'll asphyxiate if I induce vomiting. And he will pass the sample case easily in the other direction without invasive surgery."

"What?" Mallow protested. "You get your coin for cutting and poking around, don't you? Why not get paid for this?"

"As I said, it's unnecessary. I can give him a laxative and you'll most likely have what you want before sundown." He frowned at Mallow. "Besides, you still owe me for the last time I did work for you."

"I need that sample now—my employer's expecting delivery this morning, and given how many of the Bloody Thumb are hanging around this place, he's probably already on his way." She smiled up at Helik. "I promise—I'll give you my commission from this job. It's more than enough to pay for the puka and that patch-up last month."

Helik shook his head. "I'll leave the laxative."

"If you leave, I'll just slice him open myself," Mallow said. "I'll kill him. Are you ready to live with that?"

While the surgeon packed up to leave, Schmalch yelped from behind the foul-tasting rag and strained against the restraints, trying to get Helik to save him. He'd work for the chop doc the rest of his days if Helik would only take him out of this terrible warehouse.

Someone slapped the top of Schmalch's head, and Sigrin hissed in his ear, "Shut it or I'll open you up right now, Schmalchy."

"The next time you summon me, Mallow, have the coin ready up front. Along with my back-pay." Helik opened the door, stepping back with a gasp.

A karju man taller and wider than anyone in the room filled the doorway, silver-knobbed cane in one hand. He wore a lot of rich stuff—silver jewelry loaded with gems and clothes like the swish people Schmalch had seen outside the Big Island's clubs and restaurants.

"Who in the depths are you?" Rothis asked.

"Mister Marthoth," Mallow said, voice cracking. She cleared her throat. "I was just about to send for you. We have the sample."

Marthoth's eyes went around the room, pausing on Schmalch before settling on Mallow.

She chuckled nervously. "As you can see, though, we have a small problem, but I'm dealing with it. The job's binnacle let this puka—"

"Hey!" Rothis shouted. "You're not throwing me overboard, you squawking mank."

"You had a simple job." Mallow jabbed a finger at Rothis like he couldn't knock her off her chair with a single smack. "All you had to do was bring back a zoeticist who'd already stolen the sample for you. What do you bring back instead? A sample stuck inside the gudgeon, who seems to be the only competent one among you."

Rothis slapped her finger away. "You were the one who made the plan. It went keel-up first thing. The zoeticist didn't show. He didn't even steal the sample—it was still in the safe. And this scruddy thief your brother handed us didn't set off the alarm and get nabbed like he was supposed to. How is any of that my fault?"

"You left bodies in the street," Mallow yelled.

Marthoth watched the exchange silently, creases at the corners of his eyes tightening. His calm scared Schmalch more than everyone else's threats.

"You said you were a professional," Mallow continued. "You told me you had experience improvising. I paid you to do a job. If the plan drifted, you should have ridden the wave. Like a professional." She punctuated the last three words with finger jabs at Rothis.

"When this douse didn't distract the guard and the target wasn't at the backdoor I improvised," he said. "We brought you the sample. I didn't make the puka swallow it."

Mallow threw up her hands. "Dunders, all of you."

Rothis stomped around the desk. "She says she's not going to pay us a single copper. You're her boss." He poked Marthoth's rich-looking jacket. "So, I figure you owe us."

The big boss reached for an inner pocket.

"That's right," Rothis said, "we'll take our silver right now and leave this piss pot."

Marthoth removed his clenched hand from his jacket and held it close to Rothis' face. Schmalch didn't recognize the gun—so small it looked like a toy in the giant's fist—until after a chunk of skull blew out the back of the watch cap, spattering bits onto Tig's bruised face and hair. Rothis crumpled.

Schmalch wet himself.

The room went silent except for the scrabbling sound of Sigrin burrowing under his sister's desk.

Tig stared at the heap of Rothis, gore dripping off her face. Then she screamed. Her eyes went wild, and she charged Marthoth, who swung his cane overhand, cracking Tig in the forehead with its silver knob. Her knees buckled, and she collapsed into the spreading pool of blood.

Marthoth stepped over the bodies, laid his tiny gun on the table beside Schmalch, and said, "I told you to hire the Toh, Malpockey." His voice was like the rumble of distant thunder.

"I know, Mister Marthoth, but Traus said they didn't have anyone available for last night, and you know Behaani insisted it had to be last night."

"You realize I can confirm your claim."

Mallow looked down at the desk. "Right... yeah... I didn't talk to Traus. I thought it better to save your coin than waste it paying the Toh for a such a simple extraction. Those two said they were operators from Imt Hold. They passed my test. I thought they could handle it."

"You thought you'd hire some slack-jawed gudgeons to do a job on which the future prosperity of my fleet rests," Marthoth said, "and pocket the difference for yourself."

Mallow licked her lips, eyeing the little gun. "The puka did his job. He slipped in and brought the sample back. That part was a success."

"While that is some consolation," Marthoth said, "I received word that my new zoeticist was found dead in a back alley on the Big Island. The Corps are looking for whoever killed him—and one of their own. I also heard rumors concerning a dead guard at the nearby Integrated Zoetics facility."

Marthoth picked up his pistol and turned away from Mallow. "Helik, what are the options for retrieving my sample from this one's insides?"

The chop doc cleared his throat, "As I told Mallow, a laxative would pose the least risk for the patient. Were I to induce vomiting, there's a good chance he would asphyxiate. As for surgery, by the time I could get him to my boat and perform the procedure properly, the laxative would most likely have done its job."

Marthoth's eyes shifted to Schmalch. "Seems you're the only one to come out of this mess with something I want. I'm going to reward you for it."

He pulled out a little blade and Schmalch couldn't stop the whine that seeped out around the dirty cloth.

"Quiet," Marthoth said. "Don't do anything foolish."

He pulled the gag out of Schmalch's mouth and cut the restraints—not quite gently, but he wasn't as rough as Sigrin would've been.

Schmalch sat up and rubbed his wrists. "Grat," he muttered.

Marthoth crouched beside him. His head looked as big as a three-gallon keg.

"Apologies, but I don't have the patience left to wait for my property to come out your backside." Marthoth traced his little knife down the front of Schmalch's dirty shirt. "So, I'm giving you the choice. Either Dr. Ladsam cuts you open here and now, or you take a chance on choking on the sample as it comes back up."

He flicked the tip of his knife and a button flew off the shirt.

Schmalch didn't want to be cut open under any circumstances. He just wanted to do it the way Helik had said. He didn't understand why no one would just wait the day.

"It's a simple choice," Marthoth said. He flicked another button.

Schmalch's stomach churned, juices rising with his panic.

Marthoth flicked a third button and Schmalch's gut lurched. In a heave so powerful it made his eyes water, he horked and the sample flew into the air like a juggler's prop.

Marthoth caught the little black ball in midair, somehow managing to keep vomit off his jacket.

"Easier than expected," he said, studying the still-dripping sample. "Tell your brother to crawl out from under there, Malpockey, and bring me a towel."

Mallow kicked under the desk and Sigrin squealed.

"You heard him," she said.

Sigrin scrabbled out and ran into the next room.

"You, Malpockey," Marthoth said, standing to tower over her, "should close your accounts in the Haven and pack your things. *All* your things."

"W-what?" Mallow stammered.

"You are being transferred to Tehtaemah indefinitely. I have an inconsequential operation in Reilemynia that requires oversight, where you can prove to me tonight's incident is an aberration in what was a promising career."

"Tehtaemah? That scorched Duin-forsaken sea of dust?"

"The same. That's where I send people who require retraining. Fail me there, and I promise, you will die thirsty." He leaned on the desk, eye-to-eye with her. "From now on, Malpockey, when I tell you to hire the Thung Toh, you hire the Thung Toh."

"But I've never... I don't want..."

"Neither is relevant. I have a carriage waiting. Join me at my offices to discuss your new assignment."

"Now?"

"Now." Marthoth walked toward the door. "Helik, send the bill to my office."

Mallow slid off her chair and followed, her face so pale it was almost blue.

"In our absence," Marthoth told Jeho, "you and the thief clean this up."

"Yes, sir," the guard said.

Marthoth pointed at Schmalch. "If you tell anyone about this job or anything that happened here today, I will know, and I will kill you. Understood?"

Schmalch nodded until his head hurt as bad as his throat.

When Jeho left to get a cart, Schmalch rifled the bodies. Tig had nothing but a sailor's knife in her pockets, but he found his kris tucked in her boot. Relief filled him—he wasn't going to die today. His badger's luck continued when he rolled Rothis and found the shiny dagger *and* Behaani's swish pistol tucked in the small of his back. Dinnlit might straight trade both blades for a shocker for Plu, and if Schmalch found the right buyer, the gun would bring enough silver to make up for the Callas Mallow never paid him.

Jeho returned with a mop and bucket, promising to deliver the bodies to the Keepers of the Brine if Schmalch took care of the blood and bits. Schmalch agreed—he'd cleaned up bigger messes during his time at the Barnacle and was happy to avoid another visit to the Keepers. His stomach pinched and rolled the whole time he cleaned. Nothing at the Barnacle had been quite this gory.

Hours later, when he was done, Schmalch bolted out of the empty office before anyone could tell him otherwise. The warehouse was as busy as ever and Schmalch dodged workers and ponies in his sprint down the aisles of soaring shelves, his mind full of visions of a crate falling from above and crushing him before he could reach the exit. He burst into the sunset's glow still feeling like someone might grab him, tie him up, and cut him open. The sooner he put distance between himself and this warehouse, the better. Out of habit, he headed down Central Row, toward the Bitter Barnacle.

Mallow was being sent away, so there was no hope of earning a place on her crew. Sigrin would have queered that anyway, so it was just as well. Would Sigrin go with her to Tehtaemah? That would be gloss.

Ooda was mad at him. She'd told him not to come back, but maybe showing her the gun would change her mind. It was worth lots more than three Callas. But when he knocked on her door, she told him to gam off.

"I'm leaving the Haven later today when Sudii's ship leaves port," she said. A pile of bags and boxes was stacked behind her. All the furniture was gone. "*The Portentous Storm*'s crew are happy to have me onboard," she added and slammed the door.

At least he wouldn't be spending anymore coin on her.

Dinnlit probably wouldn't be at the bathhouse until morning, so Plu would have to wait for her shocker. Schmalch really wanted a drink—a whole night of drinks—but Garl wouldn't even let him in the door if he couldn't show coin. And if he showed the gun, Garl would figure some way to take it from him. Schmalch had to find someone rich enough to buy something so swish.

He found a spot below the overhang at the Order of Omatha, the shadows hiding him from the eyes of passersby hurrying to important places before the sun even showed its face.

The pistol was probably powered by opoli, which made it worth even more silver. Schmalch flicked it on just to hear the hum of the magnet coming to life. It was real swish, worth a lot of Callas. But how was he going to find a buyer willing to pay enough here on the Lower Rabble? All the toffs lived on the Big Island and the Nest, but they wouldn't buy dosh from someone like him.

Schmalch stowed the pistol. He needed to find someone local.

Distantly, he saw a dark figure cutting a ripple through the crowds, people moving from its path like some invisible wall was pushing them away. With Rothis dead, Schmalch knew only one person who could do that—Rift. She and her Duke had enough silver to buy twenty pistols like Behaani's.

"*Psst*," Schmalch ventured when her familiar black cloak neared the alley entry. "Hey Rift, over here."

Gratitude for reading

If you enjoyed *A Good Thief* **please leave a review on Goodreads or wherever you purchased this book**. Your efforts do so much to help indie authors and keep us writing.

Visit ismae.com and sign up for our email list to receive updates on our adventures. And if you're curious what happens next for Schmalch, be sure to check out the rest of the *Thung Toh Jig* series.

ACKNOWLEDGEMENTS

Our gratitude to everyone who was a part of bringing *A Good Thief* to life: Michael B. Fee, John Wikman, Kelly Wikman, Christopher J. Bennem, Eric Williams, and Eric Shallop.

A special thank you to all the reviewers who have supported us throughout this adventure. We appreciate every word you post about us and other indie authors.

Our love and gratitude to our families, who have supported us through this and so much more.

Made in the USA
Middletown, DE
29 October 2023

41490530R00061